The Avenger

His Dreamseekers

Book 4

By

Ronna M. Bacon

Isaiah 35:3-4

"Encourage the exhausted, and strengthen the feeble. Say to those with anxious heart,

"Take courage, fear not. Behold, your God will come with vengeance; The recompense of God will come, But He will save you."

NKJV

Table of Contents

Chapter 1

"Mister? Can you help us? Mister? Please? No one else will."

The young female voice stopped the man in his tracks. Dougal Hunter looked around and then down, a frown on his face as he studied the two younger people, not quite teenagers, who stood in front of him, a pleading look on the boy's face, a worried look on the girl's. Their hazel eyes matched in colour as did their auburn hair. He looked around, not quite sure that they were speaking with him.

The young girl's hand reached for his and as she grasped it, she pulled at him.

"Please? Mister? Can you help us? We need help?."

Dougal could see the sheen of tears in her eyes and frowned again.

"You need my help? Where are your parents?"

A sob came from the girl.

"They're dead. Our cousin needs your help. Please? Mister? No one else will."

Dougal sighed, not quite sure what was going on, but knowing that he could not deny them. It was ingrained in him to help those in need. He stared down at the meal that he had just picked up and then tossed it into a nearby garbage container.

"Where is she?" His deep bass voice was softened, even as his gaze shifted between the two.

"She's over here. He won't let her go. She sent us away, told us to find somewhere safe. Then we saw you. Can you help?" The young man, youth, however it was that you would describe him for he was just a young teenager if that, pulled Dougal forward.

Dougal knew better. He knew that he should not go with them, that he could be walking into something that he didn't want to. As a patrol officer for the town of Cairn, he was cautious, normally. But this time? Dougal could feel God nudging him forward, sending him with the two young people.

His hand out to stop their forward movement, his amber eyes studied the scene in front of him. A young woman, around his age, he thought, stood, arms wrapped around herself, in front of an older man. The man's arms and hands were waving in the air, and Dougal drew a deep breath as he saw the hand that reached for the lady, to drag her from the area.

With a quiet word for the two with him to stay put, Dougal strode forward, the sun reflecting off his dirty blond hair. He watched the man closely, his frown back on his face. *Lord, I have no idea what I have just walked into, but You do. You are here. Let me be the hands and feet to work for You, to protect this lady.*

His arms around the lady startled her and made her jump before she leaned back against him. She drew in a deep breath, tears of relief sparkling in her hazel eyes before she blinked rapidly and then leaned back harder against Dougal, feeling his strength and the promised protection that he offered in the tight circle of his arms.

"Can't let you out of my sight, darlin'? I wondered where you were? Are you ready to hit the road and head home?" Dougal's voice had an undertone to it that had the man stepping backwards, his eyes hard and angry, before he reached for the lady again.

Dougal's hand came up and he brushed the man's hand to one side even as he swept the lady behind him.

"Not happening, my friend. She's with me." Dougal shoved at her to get her moving backwards towards the trees where he had left the two younger people. "Darlin', let's move. We have places to go and people to see."

The man threatened and yelled as they moved away from him, the violent manner of his actions bringing a deeper frown and more concern to Dougal. He had no idea what he had just walked into but he feared for the lady with him.

Able at last to turn, he reached for her hand, finding hers clutching at him as he walked rapidly, heading away from the young people, watching as they followed him. Reaching his truck, his finger hit the button on the key fob and he literally lifted the lady onto the seat, seeing the other two running to climb into the back seat. A smile played around his mouth even as he turned, searching for the man and

—

not finding him. Dougal sighed. Lord? I have no idea what this means or who she is or who he was.

Heading away from the area, Dougal searched for somewhere that he could pull over safely, not familiar with the town of Lakeview. A friend had moved there, a fellow officer, and he had headed that way on an extended vacation.

"Please? Can you stop? Let us out?" The soft voice from the lady beside him caught his attention. "Please?"

"Sure. Look, it's time for lunch. Let me find somewhere I can grab something for us all and then a place to eat. Then, we'll talk." Dougal knew that they had to, he just wasn't sure if she would.

Dougal and the young man headed for the local restaurant, intent on finding their food.

"I'm Dougal Hunter. And you would be? I like to know the names of my friends." Dougal grinned down at the young man.

"We're friends?" The young man looked up at him, wonder on his face, hiding the fear for a moment.

"That we are. I don't walk away from people who need my help. A good friend would have my head if I did that." Dougal stood in line, eyes watchful, not seeing anything that concerned him but he could feel that niggling sensation at the back of his neck, knowing that he was in danger and just didn't know why. He knew his friend from childhood, Holly Carmichael, would tell him to help and ask him just why he hadn't if he refused.

—

"I'm Camm O'Shea. My sister is Cori. And our cousin is McKala. Thank you for helping her." Camm reached for the tray of drinks. "Thanks, mister. We haven't eaten in a couple of days. McKala had her money stolen and she hasn't been able to replace it."

Dougal choked as he tried to speak. *How did this happen, Lord? Thank You that I am here, able to be Your hands in this.*

"She did? I have a friend here who can help. And he has more friends that can help."

Dougal crumpled the paper from his meal, reaching for all the garbage and then pausing before he opened the door. He had watched the three cousins, seeing the love that they shared with one another but also seeing the worry underlying their looks and in their words.

"Stay put. I'll be right back and we'll talk. McKala? Do you hear me?" Dougal was hesitant to get out of the vehicle, knowing that McKala might just take off and he just didn't want her to do that, ever. He didn't know that his heart had already been claimed by McKala.

McKala watched as Dougal walked towards the garbage container, her prayer of thankfulness rising, but she also felt fear. That man was around, she could feel him. He had haunted her steps for months now. She had been on the move, pulling her young charges from school and schooling them herself, desperate to escape him and not knowing how to or who to turn to. They had wandered the province until her car had broken down outside of Lakeview.

McKala had been unable to get it repaired, her money disappearing that same day. Forced to live on the streets, they had scrounged for food. Now, she had hope. Someone had stepped in. She studied Dougal and his height and strength, remembering how safe she had felt when his arms had come around her.

A sound from Camm had her head turning to him before she heard a cry from Cori. When she looked forward, she saw the vehicle heading for Dougal at high speed and then saw how he launched himself sideways, the truck missing him by mere inches before it kept on going and disappeared from sight.

Dougal rolled as he landed and then was on his feet, running for his own truck and jumping in. He felt McKala's hand on his arm before he turned, seeing the shock on her face.

"Did he really do that?" McKala could barely speak.

"He did. And we will talk, McKala. I mean that. Right now, I need to put in a report on this." His hand went up at her protest. "I'm sorry, McKala. I need to. I'm a police officer and that was attempted murder. And you will tell me why he's after you." Dougal winced at how forceful his words were but he was scared, he had to admit, that something would happen to one of his companions, and that he just could not live with.

McKala sighed. "I know. I will. It's just that I tried to get someone to believe me when it first started and I was told that I was imagining it all. Only I'm not. Thank God that you were not hurt."

Dougal watched in fascination as her auburn curls moved with her head actions as she turned to comfort her cousins. *I have no idea where this is heading, Lord, but You do. Help me to protect these three. I know my friend here will help as will his friends. Only, I have no idea what I just walked into. She's terrified, that much I know, and trying hard to hide it from her family. Only that's not working. These two are too savvy for that to happen.*

Chapter 2

Standing with his hands jammed into his jeans pockets, Dougal watched as the patrol officer walked back towards him. Camm was beside him, as close as he could stand, not willing to wait with the ladies as Dougal had suggested. Instead, he had chosen, no, wanted to be as close to the tall man beside whom he was standing as he could be. He missed his father desperately. Camm loved his cousin and appreciated her care but he just needed a male figure that he could talk with. He prayed that Dougal would not leave them. Camm had caught a look on Dougal's face when he looked at McKala similar to how his father had looked at his mother and prayed harder.

"Dougal? What now?"

"What now?" Dougal rested a hand on Camm's shoulder, finding the youth leaning into it. "We finish speaking with this officer. Then we find somewhere to crash for the night." He paused, his hand rubbing at his face. "Just a thought, Camm. Do you three have any luggage?"

Camm shook his head. "All our stuff disappeared from McKala's car before we could get back to it. We still don't understand how she lost her money. She never set her purse down, not that she can remember." Camm groaned. "The only time was when she had to use a pay phone. She was distracted for a moment and had turned away from where she

———

13

had set it on the table beside it. I thought I saw someone there but there were people around us and I wasn't sure."

"That's when that likely happened. It just takes a few seconds for someone experienced in thefts like that to take something and be lost in the crowd." Dougal looked up as he heard new footsteps and frowned for a moment before his hand was out to shake Evan Brant's, a friend and former undercover police officer.

"Evan? You're here?" Dougal looked surprised and then pleased.

"I am. I was heading home and saw the commotion. Up to no good again, Dougal?" Evan grinned at his friend even as his eyes shifted to Camm and then raised to watch McKala and Cori as they too had approached.

"Me? Up to no good? More than likely that would be you. How's Flannery?"

"She is well. Looking forward to your visit." Evan caught the slight shake of Dougal's head and knew that they would be talking and soon. "Who are your friends, Dougal?"

"This is Camm O'Shea." Dougal turned to look for the ladies, a hand out to draw McKala to his side, her own hand clutching Cori's. "And this is McKala O'Shea and her cousin and Camm's sister, Cori. They've run into a bit of difficulty in the last couple of days. Do Eunice and Everett still take in waifs and strays?"

"They do, but we have a cabin on our property that they could use. It's small and compact. Flannery insisted that we needed it. They're welcome to it if they wish."

"We'll see, Evan. At least we'll come out for a while, I think. Let me talk it over with McKala. Tell Flannery that I'll be around at some point." Dougal once again gave a slight shake of his head.

Evan sighed to himself. *Another friend,* he thought, *caught up in an adventure and from the look on Dougal's face, he is not walking away from this lady and her cousins. His heart is already taken, isn't it, Lord? And we need to figure out how to keep him safe and alive and to protect these three as well.*

"Sure. You know where we are. It's been a while since you've been around."

"That it has. Holly and Lincoln said to say hi as did Doc and his family."

Evan nodded, spoke to Dougal for another few moments and then headed home to find his bride of a few months. Flannery would want to know what was going on. Only he had no idea just what that was.

McKala stared after Evan, a puzzled look on her face, as she listened to Dougal finish speaking with the officer. Dougal in turn watched her closely as he waited for her to speak. Camm and Cori headed back for his truck, whispers between them as they threw glances at McKala and Dougal, puzzled that she allowed him to hold her hand. That was not her, they knew.

"McKala?" Dougal waited patiently, knowing that at some point she would speak.

—

15

"Your friend, Dougal? He offered to let us stay at his place? He doesn't know us." McKala was puzzled.

"No, he doesn't. He knows me and knows that I would not be helping you three if I had sensed anything off or odd or wrong about this situation. There is not, other than you have found yourselves in an adventure and somehow pulled me in." His free hand went up as her mouth opened to protest. "No, it's fine, McKala. Let me help you discover who it is that is tracking you. There is a reason for that. For one thing, I can't walk away from anyone in trouble. Nor can my friends, including Evan, who by the way was a police officer. Secondly, there is something about you and your cousins that makes me want to help you and relieve the stress and burdens that you have been carrying."

Dougal turned her towards the truck, leading her that way and then tucking her inside. He stood for a moment, scanning the area out of habit before he shook his head and then climbed in himself. Biting at his lip, he felt uncertain, knowing from Camm that they needed clothing and other supplies, personal stuff as he thought of it, and wasn't quite sure how to approach McKala.

"McKala? Camm said that your luggage was stolen?"

McKala sighed, her eyes staring out the windshield, her hands rubbing at her arms, not quite certain on the tall, very good-looking man who was watching her. She saw a look in his eyes that paused her and warmed her heart. *Lord? Has someone finally come along to help me, to find out who it has been all these years? If so, thank You.*

"It was. And I can't replace it."

Dougal nodded before he pulled away, heading for the outskirts of town and a little shopping mall where he knew that they could find what they wanted. McKala stared at the store and then at him, her mouth open to speak before Dougal's hand was wrapped around hers and she heard his prayers, for her, for Camm and Cori, for a quick end to their trouble, for protection and peace.

Chapter 3

Dougal stood in the store, watching with amusement as Camm couldn't decide if he wanted to stay with Dougal or head off with either Cori or McKala. His eyes raised to watch McKala as she moved through the clothing section, finding bargains that he didn't even know existed for the three of them. She had protested when he had approached her while she had stood by his truck, not sure what to do.

"McKala? What do you need?" Dougal had studied her face, compassion on his as she had hesitated. "It's okay. You need clothes. Find what you want." A hand went up as her mouth opened to protest. "No, I mean it. Find what you want and what you need. It's okay. I can do this for you." He simply reached to hug her before he turned to the store, her hand in his as he walked that way, Cori and Camm flanking them.

Camm approached Dougal, a worried look on his face.

"She won't get everything we need, Dougal. I just know that she won't."

"She will. Listen, if you see anything that you would like or see Cori or McKala looking at something and putting it back, bring it to me. Okay?" Dougal grinned at Camm as he looked up first at him and then at the ladies and then back at him before a grin lit up his own face. "Can you do that?"

—

"I can." Camm was off again, bringing items of clothing and dumping them in the cart that Dougal had beside him.

"Camm?" Dougal waited as Camm turned back to him, Cori coming up to stand tight to his side. "You need swimsuits. All three of you."

"We do?" Cori was puzzled herself, not sure what Dougal was meaning.

"You do. Evan? My friend? He lives on the lake. We'll be able to go swimming there. And if you stay there even for a few days, you'll get to play in the lake." He grinned as their faces lit up with delight. "So, off you two go. Find swimsuits for all of you. And anything else that you think you might need to have fun in the water."

They turned, ready to run, before he spoke quietly again. He watched with amusement as they heeded his words of admonition and walked away as rapidly as they could without running.

McKala turned from the store shelves, looking in despair at the full cart. It was too much, she thought, before her head raised. She could feel herself being watched, as she had been so much in the past few months and shivered at the fear that chased up and down her spine. That McKala was worried deeply about her charges was a given. She just didn't know how to protect them. Running away and traveling around the province obviously had not worked.

Dougal caught the look of fear that flickered across McKala's face and turned, searching the people around her. He didn't see anyone that caused concern but he knew someone was there. He could feel the prickles on the back of his neck that warned him of danger. He had learned to listen to his sense of danger. Holly, his long-time friend, had often teased him about that but when she and Lincoln had gone through their adventure as it was termed, she had learned exactly what he meant.

"McKala? Everything okay?" Dougal's hand on her arm paused her forward walk, his head tilting to watch her.

McKala shrugged. "I'm not sure any more, Dougal. It's been hard. The kids were only small when their parents died in a flash flood. The road that they were on should have been safe and wasn't. I was their only next of kin and had agreed that I would raise them, never expecting it to happen."

"How old were they?" Dougal didn't move his hand, watching as Camm and Cori had approached and stopped, worry on their faces as they watched their cousin.

"It's been seven years, Dougal. Camm was five, Cori four. Too young to lose their parents." McKala blinked rapidly to clear the tears before a frown covered her face. "He's here, Dougal. God help us. He's found us again."

Dougal nodded and then gently led her to the cashier, gathering the bags with the help of Camm and Cori before he pointed to the doors.

"Let's head out, McKala. We need to talk." He shook his head as she looked up in protest. "We'll talk, love. We'll talk. I will not walk away from you. First, as a police officer, I just can't do that. I have to find this person or persons and set you free of the terror and fear that you three have been living under. Secondly? I just can't walk away from a beautiful lady in trouble. That's not who I am or what I do."

Dougal stood for a moment, his hand on the back of his truck cap, watching as McKala hesitated to climb in. He hid a grin as he saw Camm trying hard to persuade her to just get in. Cori reached to hug him, surprising him, before she ran to climb into the truck. He sighed. What did I just go and do, Lord? I shouldn't have but they needed these things. His phone vibrated and he pulled it out, a smile on his face as he read his father's message.

He looked up and then back at the message, before sending off a reply, simply stating that he had found a young lady and her two charges in difficulty and had helped them out. Yes, he replied, that meant spending money and he thanked his father for forwarding on the funds that he needed, without asking why. Dougal's father's had set up a charity, just to help provide supplies and clothing for those in need, without putting a limit on his son's spending. His trust in Dougal had been proven many times over.

McKala watched as Dougal climbed behind the wheel and then just sat, his fingers tapping at the wheel.

"Dougal? If it's too much, we can return things." McKala drew in a deep, shuddering breath, her emotions raw. She had been on her own for years, losing her own parents in a drunk driving accident while in college, the other driver having well over the legal limit of alcohol and drugs in his system. He had walked away with serious injuries, not even caring that he had devastated a family. McKala knew in her heart that they needed all that they had bought, not realizing that Dougal had purchased items with Camm's help that were what they had wanted. She just didn't know how to decide what to return.

Dougal shook his head, before he looked over at her, knowing that the two youngsters as his father termed them were watching him and then McKala.

"It's okay, McKala. We don't have to return anything. And if there is more that you need, we can do that." He shook his head at her once more. "Let me explain. My Dad has a service program that funds supplies and whatnot for people in need just like you. He doesn't place a limit on what I spend when I do, knowing that I have assessed the situation and have moved forward as God would have me to. That's how we are the hands and feet for God."

McKala stared at him for a moment before she blinked rapidly. She could hear Camm and Cori whispering to one another, happy smiles on their faces, before she nodded. The tears that clogged her throat prevented her from speaking. Dougal simply reached to wipe a tear from her cheek that had escaped before he started the truck and drove away, heading just where he wasn't sure. All he knew that that he didn't want to let this lady escape him, or the two youngsters, God willing.

Chapter 4

McKala studied the tall, handsome man, her age she figured, as he walked back from yet another store, Camm and Cori as tight to him as they could get. She shook her head as she noticed Cori grasping Dougal's hand. They are happy, she thought, happier than they have been in years. What is it about this man that caused that?

Walking away from where she had been leaning against the truck, McKala watched as Cori ran towards her, to throw her arms around her cousin in a tight hug.

"He's so nice, McKala."

Sighing to herself, McKala just nodded. He would be gone from their lives soon, that much she knew or was it afraid of? She suddenly wished life was different, that she wasn't on the run with Camm and Cori, didn't have to watch for someone coming after her, and could just date and maybe find the man that her parents had prayed for, just for her. She figured that would never happen.

Dougal looked up with a grin, happiness wafting through him. He studied McKala for a moment and then prayed for her. Just how to pray, that was the question, but he knew that God would understand. He could feel the danger fast approaching her and just didn't know how much that

—

she would let him into her life and let him keep her safe.

"Here, McKala. A phone for you." Dougal extended his hand, the phone held out for her.

McKala stared at him and that at it.

"I can't take it." McKala was shaking her head.

Dougal studied it, studied her, and then just simply reached for her hand, folding it around the phone.

"It's okay, McKala. I just added it to my plan. It's okay. Really, it is." He reached for her other hand and walked towards another store.

McKala pulled him to a stop, a frown on her face that changed to a perplexed look.

"I don't understand, Dougal." Her eyes sought his face, finding a peace on it that she didn't feel.

"I know, McKala. We need to talk, I know." Dougal bit at his lip, suddenly uncertain, even though he had peace from God that this was a move to make. "You need someone to protect you and Camm and Cori. I would like to step in and do that. I am offering you my name and my home to do that." He looked past her for a moment, seeing the worried look on Cori's face but the look on Camm's face stopped his gaze there. *Camm understands, doesn't he, Lord? I see that look that I see far too often. A loss of innocence in a child. This should never happen.* "I am a police officer in a town named Cairn. You would have the protection of the members of that force. The town will look out for you and Camm and Cori. That's what they do, watch out for one another.

But I will not push you. If you say that you don't want to or need time, we walk away from here. I can find someone for you three to stay within Cairn, if that is what you wish."

McKala stared up at him, thinking how tall he was. *This is what You planned, Lord? For Dougal to walk in like this? To help us? But how do I do this? Do I take him up on his offer or do I walk away, endangering Camm and Cori even more?* She then turned her eyes to Camm and then to Cori, seeing their wish in their eyes and the happiness that was fluttering across their faces. *How do I do this, Lord? McKala's drifted to the Bible, to the stories of ladies entering arranged marriages and then sighed. This is Your will and way for me, isn't it, Lord?*

McKala turned to study the two youngsters, finding hope and worry on Cori's face and hope and peace and understanding on Camm's. *Is this the way, Lord, that You want me to walk? To accept Dougal's proposal, at least for now?*

Turning back to Dougal, she studied him, seeing his character in his face and eyes, and knowing in her heart that he would do everything he could to protect. Her only thought was that she may not be able to walk away from him when she was finished with whatever it was. She slowly nodded, taking the hand that he reached back out for her, letting him lead her into the jewelry store.

———

Chapter 5

Evan and Flannery exchanged glances before looking back at Dougal. A frown covered Evan's face for a moment. Flannery simply reached to hug Dougal and then McKala, an arm around her as she led her into the cabin.

"I'm Flannery and Evan and I had an adventure. He's a retired officer as well." Flannery studied her. "I know. You're unsure of yourself. Dougal's a good man. I don't know him all that well, but Evan has been a friend for a few years. Now, about you."

McKala sighed, something she thought she had done a lot of that day. Cori hugged her cousin, apprehension on her face that McKala would run and take them with her. And she didn't want to do that. She was young, tired of running, and Dougal had become a friend and big brother already. She didn't want to lose that.

Blinking rapidly, McKala finally nodded. She was ready, she thought. She studied the diamond ring that Dougal had chosen for her. She had opened her mouth to protest and then stopped as she watched his face. He needed to do this.

Flannery pulled her into a bedroom and then opened the closet door, pulling out a dress bag.

"Here. My dress will fit you, if you want to use it." Flannery watched her carefully, an eye on Cori as she gently felt the dress.

Cori felt hope rising in her, a hope that she had not had for years. She knew that McKala had tried but it had been hard for all of them. McKala had not shared all of what was going on, that much Cori had figured out.

Biting at her lip, McKala studied the dress, praying for the peace that she needed. She nodded at long last, her eyes on Cori, who grinned and then hugged her tight.

Dougal stood, his eyes on the cabin, hearing Camm and Evan talking, knowing that Evan was drawing Camm out about what had happened. He reached for his phone, knowing that his father would be on the line.

"Dougal?" Duncan's voice held a question, one that he would not ask.

"Dad? What are you and Mom and Deveney up to tomorrow? Any chance that you're free and could head this way?"

Duncan shared a look with Abigayle before he shrugged.

"We're free. You're at Evan's?"

"I am, Dad." Dougal drew a deep breath. "I could use you three for support. That lady and her cousins?"

"McKala, you said her name was?"

"That's right, Dad." Dougal stared as McKala moved towards him, an arm out to sweep her to him, before he turned them away from the cabin and towards the dock. "It's just that we've decided to marry and I would like you to be here."

———

Duncan shared a look with his wife and then his daughter, before his eyes slid closed. *He's really doing this, isn't he, Lord? And we have to support him. If he's prayed about it, and I know he has, then that's what we do.*

"We'll head up there today, Dougal. We're all here." Duncan prayed with his son before he set his phone down, his eyes on it.

"He's really doing that, Dad?" Deveney rubbed her hands on her legs, not sure what Dougal was up to.

"He is and we support him." Duncan shared a look with his wife and daughter. "He has prayed and I know that he would not go forward with this if he had not."

McKala watched Duncan closely, seeing the peace that he had, and then prayed for that. She had made a decision, not having God tell her no, and intended to move forward with it.

"Dougal? What about that man?"

"Him? I have passed on what information I had on him to Brownie, a friend on the force here. He'll watch for him, but it would not surprise me to see him go into hiding somewhere." Dougal just stood, his arm still around the lady who had already claimed his heart. He was just reluctant to admit that.

Chapter 6

Abigayle studied her son the next morning, reaching to hug him, holding on a little bit longer than she normally would. Their relationship was changing, she knew, and well it should. She stepped back, her hands on his arms, studying him. *When did he grow up on us, Lord? He is a man, well established in his career, totally dedicated to You, and now taking a step of faith.*

"Mom?" Dougal's voice held a question.

"You're sure, son?"

"I am, Mom. I can't walk away. Not from any of them. They need me." Dougal blinked for a moment, his emotions raw, before he smiled. "And I need them. I know what Holly meant."

"What? That you can keep McKala?" Deveney reached to hug her brother. "And where are they?"

"Down by the lake. Flannery is with them. Evan had to head over to the other house for a bit." Dougal turned as his father's hand touched his shoulder and he heard his father praying for him. He looked up, to find his father's eyes narrowed as he studied Dougal before he nodded and then hugged his son.

"Where's your lady, son? And do you have all your plans made?"

Dougal paused and then nodded.

—

"We do, Dad. This is hard for her. Camm and Cori are happy, but McKala is worried about the danger that she brings to me."

Deveney laughed. "And she doesn't think about the danger that you are in every day?"

Dougal simply shook his head at his sister.

"She does, but this is different, sis. Let's find my lady and the two youngsters." Dougal walked away, an arm around his sister, leaving his parents staring after him.

"He's different today, Abigayle."

"He is. He's taking a huge step, love, and still not sure if it's correct. He's waited, never dating, until now. He'll be second guessing himself more than likely." His mother walked towards Flannery who stood waiting near the cabin. "Flannery, my dear. So lovely to see you. What can I do to help?"

Late that afternoon, Dougal stood, Evan beside him, staring down at the envelope that he had just opened. Photos of McKala and the youngsters as he termed them fell to the ground before he stooped to pick them up. Evan reached for them.

"This was when?" Evan frowned, knowing that the photos were from his town.

"Yesterday. When we were shopping. Before we came out here." Dougal shook his head. "And I have to tell her."

Evan looked around him, a slight grin on his face.

"You just did, Dougal."

Dougal's eyes closed briefly before he looked to his left. McKala stood there, her eyes on the photos.

"More photos? They've done that lately. The ones that I had received were in my car and disappeared with all my things."

"They did?" Evan and Dougal shared a look before Dougal's arm came around McKala and drew her close to him. "Hiding the evidence, I would think."

"Isn't that what they always do?" McKala stared out across the lake, arms folded across her abdomen.

Dougal studied her in turn, thinking how beautiful she was in Flannery's wedding dress. Nerves had hit both of them as they exchanged their vows, searching one another's face, puzzlement in their eyes. His hands had been shaking as he placed the wedding band, knowing that he would never walk away from her. He would die before he did that, and that was something that worried him. Neither knew who was after McKala or why.

McKala studied Dougal now, her eyes puzzled.

"Dougal? What now? They won't stop, will they? And how do I protect Camm and Cori? I can't lose them." McKala was almost in tears at that thought.

Dougal simply swept her into a hug, his head bowed as he prayed for them all. Evan watched, an arm coming out to draw Flannery to him. It had been hard enough for them, but it had only been the two of them, well and Lydia, his life-long friend whose parents lived next door. He could not understand how difficult it was for Dougal, not really. Both men had seen too much on the streets, Evan a retired undercover officer.

"We will do our best to keep all of us safe." Dougal's chin rested on her head. "We have to trust God, McKala darlin'. He has ultimate control."

"I know, Dougal. I know. I just wish it was different." McKala's head rested against his chest, hearing his promise to protect her with every fibre of his being with each beat of his heart.

Chapter 7

Dougal hesitated two days later, staring at the lake in front of him. Evan and Flannery were around, at least that was what he thought. Camm and Cori were with Everett, somewhere he imagined, more than likely out on the lake. They had taken to Everett and Eunice, treating them like their long-lost grandparents and then had taken to the lake, Everett's dog, Sam, a willing participant in their fun.

McKala watched Dougal from where she stood just inside the back door of the little cabin that they had been using. They needed to talk and soon, she knew. Dougal was due back on duty in a few days and just what that meant for her, she was unsure of. Dougal turned to face her, stopping suddenly as he heard a slight sound. He searched and then with one foot lifted in preparation to taking a running step towards her, his body flew backwards, to land heavily on the ground. He lay still, unmoving, blood on his chest, his arms and legs in awkward sprawled positions.

McKala screamed, her instincts telling her to run towards Dougal, the shout that had died on his lips driving her to slam the door and lock it and then desperately search for a hiding place. She spun in a circle for a moment before running for the bathroom, yanking open the door to the linen closet and crouching down inside, in as small a heap as she could, the door swinging shut behind her.

———

33

Evan's body whipped around from where he stood at the end of his dock, his eyes searching for who had screamed. His feet pounded along the dock and then dug into the dirt path, even as he shouted for Flannery to call for Dooley. Flannery nodded, already flying for the cabin. Something had happened, that much she knew, and that had been McKala who had screamed.

Sliding to a halt, his eyes on the trees surrounding the area, Evan frowned. He couldn't see anyone but something had happened. He turned towards the cabin as he heard Flannery.

"Dooley's on his way as is Daniel." Her hand suddenly slapped across her mouth as she stifled a scream. "Evan! Dougal! He's hurt! And where is McKala?"

Evan spun once more, feeling that was all that he had done in the last few minutes before he charged across the area to drop to his knees beside his friend, a hand out to feel for Dougal's pulse. He felt Flannery's hand on his shoulder before she was on her knees on the other side, towels that she had grabbed jammed against the bloody mess on Dougal's chest.

"Is he alive?" Flannery's voice was barely a whisper, she was that scared for their friend.

"He is, but not by much. Paramedics?"

"They're coming." Flannery looked behind her. "This is when we could use Everett, only he needs to be with Camm and Cori. Eunice was away with Lydia today."

Evan stood back for a moment, watching Dougal closely as he was worked over in a frantic motion, not seeing Dooley pouring the saline solution over his hands to remove the blood stains. Flannery's arm was around him as she looked around.

"Where is McKala, Evan? Did they get her?"

Dooley shot a look around before he pointed towards the cabin.

"In there?"

Evan nodded even as he reached for his keys, striding rapidly towards the cabin, unlocking the door. Dooley moved in front of him, motioning for him to stay put. Evan sighed, knowing that he had to and suddenly wishing that he was an officer again and could go in and help to search.

Dooley stood for a moment, his eyes puzzled before his head tilted at the slight sound. Following it, he reached for the door to the linen closet, opening it slowly, his eyes dropping to McKala.

McKala looked up in terror, recognizing Dooley and then surged to her feet and past him, running towards Dougal, not sure if he was even alive. She ignored Evan's outstretched hand as he reached to stop her, her pace picking up as she saw the stretcher rushing towards the paramedic rig. She was up and into it before anyone could say a word, startling the paramedics who stared at one another and then at her before one reached to remove her.

Dooley's quiet comment to let her be stopped the men, who turned to study him before they nodded. The stretcher loaded, one paramedic hopped up, his eyes on Dougal even as he reached to continue his assessment and treatment.

"He's alive?" McKala's quiet question barely broke through the noise that sounded around her.

The paramedic nodded, his eyes briefly meeting hers.

"He is. You're related?"

"He's my husband." Tears clogged her voice for a moment. "We were just married. Two days ago. He saved me from someone and then offered to help me. Please, Lord, don't let him die."

The man shot her another look, shock on his face before he covered it. He wasn't quite sure if what she said was the truth but it wasn't his place to decide that. His duty was to the man in front of him and trying to keep him alive long enough to reach better help.

Chapter 8

McKala refused to move from beside Dougal's stretcher, no matter the number of requests from the staff. The physician looked at her and then at Dooley, moving briefly away from his assessment to speak with him.

"Dooley? What is going on? We can't get her to move away." The physician was frustrated at the very least.

"No, she stays, Doc. He saved her from an abduction a few days ago and then married her to keep her safe. This is what happened. She needs to be with him." Dooley's hand went up as the physician protested. "If you won't agree, then I want to speak with the head of the hospital. She stays. I stay. Both of them are under police protection and this is one way." Dooley refused to budge, instead walking to stand beside McKala, a hand under her arm to help her stand upright.

The physician, looking angry, returned to work on Dougal. He stood back at last before he nodded. The surgeon who had entered spoke with him before he approached McKala, his attitude different than the physician.

"Mrs. Hunter?" His voice startled McKala and she stared at him in fright, her eyes huge in her white face. "Can you come with me for a moment? No, we won't leave the room. Just over in this corner. I need to speak with you for a moment as to what we need to do for your husband?"

McKala refused to take her eyes from Dougal, hating that he was lying there, hurt because of her. And she didn't know if he would live. She saw the grayness of his skin, the blue that was beginning to show on his lips.

"Mrs. Hunter? McKala? We're taking Dougal to surgery in just a few minutes. The bullet has hit near the heart. How close and how much damage? That we will assess once we're in there." He went on to speak of what would happen in surgery, what they hoped and what they feared to find, what the next course would be.

McKala nodded and reached for the clipboard holding the consents for surgery that she needed to sign. She could not control the tears, feeling Dooley's arm around her before she scrawled her name and then was gone, back beside Dougal, his hand in hers, her other hand on his face. She was deeply afraid that he would not survive the surgery or be crippled and just how she would live with that, she was not sure.

Eunice approached, stopping beside Dooley. He had reached out to her, asking her to come, before he had called Duncan, simply stating that Dougal had been hurt and was heading for surgery. McKala needed them.

Duncan had asked few questions, knowing that Dooley was not saying a lot, and simply stated that they were on their way. Was someone with McKala and Camm and Cori? Dooley assured him that there was.

McKala sat not moving, her eyes glued to the doors that lead to the hallway to the surgical suite. Camm and Cori sat as tight to her as they could get, their arms wrapped around her. Both had tear stains on their faces. McKala was not crying, at least not physically. Her tears ran down into her heart and flooded it. She was afraid, no terrified, that Dougal was dead and that they wouldn't tell her.

Flannery sat beside Cori, an arm around the young girl, fervent prayers being raised quickly. She had seen the look on Evan's face and knew that he feared for his friend. Just who it had been, that was uncertain, she knew.

Camm looked up as he felt an arm on his shoulders and then was swept into Abigayle's hug. He clung to her, hearing her whispered prayers before he sat back.

"You're here?"

"Of course we are. Dougal needs us and so do the three of you. You're family. We could do nothing else." Duncan crouched down in front of him, a hand on his arm. "We can't be anywhere other than here." He reached to hug McKala. "Any word?"

"Not yet. I thought that they would." McKala was suddenly on her feet, brushing past them to head for the surgeon. "Doctor?"

The surgeon, Paul by name, paused. It had been a struggle, he had to admit to himself, almost losing Dougal on numerous occasions. He had felt

---

the prayers of the people as he worked, intervening in Dougal's life and death. Dougal should not be alive, that much he knew. The bullet had been too close to the heart sac, just missing it by such a slight margin. His team had worked together, worked to save a young man's life, and had succeeded.

"He's alive, McKala." His hand went out to steady her as Duncan's arm came around her. Camm and Cori stood close to her, watching him with fear and hope on their faces. "It took a lot of work and hunting but we managed to stop the bleeding. He's in Recovery right now, McKala. Then, he'll be moved to an ICU bed. How long he remains there depends on how well he does. Do you have any questions?"

McKala shook her head, struggling to control her tears, her arms around Camm and Cori.

"I need to see him. Please? Can I see him?"

Chapter 9

Two days later, McKala stood, her arms wrapped around herself, at the window in the waiting room. Her gaze was not focused on the outside. Paul had been around, studying her closely before he had moved to speak with her. He was surprised to find her on her own, something unusual in the last two days.

McKala had simply nodded as he spoke. Dougal was not awakening, not like he should be, and that concerned them. Did he have a known medical history that she could share with them? Paul had asked.

"I don't know, Paul. I'm sorry. He saved me from someone, we married two days later. We haven't had a chance to talk about anything." She had refused to look at him, not wanting to see condemnation on his face.

Paul had simply nodded, thinking that had been the case, given what he had been told.

"Do I have your permission to speak with his parents?" At her nod, he had sighed to himself. *This is not easy, Lord, not at all. I saw what Evan, Tag, and Shay went through, what little I was involved in that. They were all prayed through their adventures. This is what has to happen. And I fear for the lives of these two young people, and for Camm and Cori.*

———

41

Dooley walked across to stand beside her. He was here in his official capacity and he didn't like that at all. He stared out the window, watching as the drizzle became heavier. Duncan had approached him, asking what they could do to help. Was there someone somewhere that they could contact? Dooley had shaken his head. At the moment, they had little information. McKala had been unable to provide much and she refused to let him talk to Camm and Cori. They didn't need that, she had maintained, and likely didn't know much at all. She would be the one talking to them. He had no choice but to agree.

"Dooley?" McKala finally spoke, a hand rubbing at her face. "Any news?"

"I'm sorry, McKala. There is not. We don't have enough information." He paused, not sure how to phrase what he needed to ask. "Can you work with a police artist to get us a sketch?"

McKala nodded, before she handed him the paper that she had been worrying in her hand.

"I can do better. This is him. I found it in the newspaper online. I wasn't searching for him but it showed up. I can't explain it. It has to be God that did it."

Dooley reached for it, studying her for a moment, before he unrolled it. He froze, knowing that he knew the man and just what he was capable of. If he was after McKala and it appeared that he was, she was in deep danger and so were Camm and Cori. The man would not hesitate to use them against her.

"Do you know who this is?"

McKala's head shook as she turned to face him.

"I have no idea. I don't know why he would be after me. I have nothing that he wants. Nor do Camm or Cori. What little we had? That was in my car. And that disappeared." She brushed by him, tears on her face, as she almost ran for Dougal's room.

Dooley stared after her and then down at the photo, hearing footsteps stop beside him. Evan peered at the paper.

"Him?"

"Him. And she has no idea why."

Evan's breath was drawn in sharply, sounding loud in the silence of the room.

"And that's not good. Dooley has become involved in something that he will not walk away from."

"That's true. You three were like that." Dooley studied Evan, knowing that his friend would not step away from Dougal.

"How do we help?" Evan rubbed at his face, knowing that he had to call someone but just who that was, he wasn't sure.

"We'll need to talk to Duncan and his family. I just don't know how to do that, not knowing what this man wants from McKala."

"She has nothing?"

"No. She said that everything that the three of them had disappeared from her car. That's sad, you know."   Dooley walked away, leaving Flannery staring after him and then at Evan.

"Evan?" Flannery's voice reached to him and then she walked into his hug. "What's going on?"

"McKala found out the name of the man who has been after her and found his picture. It's not good, Flannery. Not at all."

"We didn't think it would be. How can we help? And have you contacted Emma?"

"Not at yet. I need to talk to McKala before I do. And that's going to be difficult."

Chapter 10

Three days later, McKala stood at Dougal's bedside, her hand on his, the other hand on his cheek. She could feel the roughness of the stubble on his cheek and that saddened her. She knew that he liked to be clean shaven. He had told her that with a grin on his face. The sounds of the equipment surrounding him hit her ears and frightened her. He should have been awake, Paul stated, and he just didn't know why he wasn't. She studied the whiteness, almost grayness, of his face and the faint blue of his lips and heard the shallow breathing that was aided by the ventilator.

Abigayle was at her side, an arm around her daughter-in-law. She hadn't gotten to know her, not yet. There just had not been time. She watched her closely, seeing the sorrow on McKala's face but also the underlying fear. Holly had been in touch, asking what she and Lincoln could do and could they just talk to anyone for them, just to bring in help? Abigayle had hesitated and then said, no, that decision had to be McKala's, unless it came to the point that someone had to step in. Holly had sighed and stated that it was at that point already. Dougal would want that, she was sure. Abigayle had smiled and then assured Holly they would do just that, once McKala had agreed. Holly had sighed again, knowing this was the case.

"McKala? Has Paul been around?"

McKala nodded.

"He was, really early. He said he was heading into surgery today for the day." She blinked rapidly. "I hate this, Abigayle. I don't cry and I feel like all I have done in the last few days is just that."

"God understands, dear. He bottles those tears." Abigayle's prayer reached to McKala's heart and she sighed.

"Abigayle, what do I do if he doesn't wake up? How do I go on? And how do I tell Camm and Cori that? Camm has been thrilled to have Dougal in his life. He's needed that."

Abigayle's eyes were on her son, watching as his own eyes had opened and fastened on McKala. They were clear and that made her frown. Where was the pain that should be in them?

McKala jumped as she felt a hand on top of her and stared down at it. Dougal's other hand rested on top of hers, the rose gold wedding band reflecting back the overhead lights. That shouldn't have happened, now should it? Her eyes raised to his face, finding him watching her, unable to speak with his voice, but his eyes spoke for him.

"Dougal?" She was in shock, to put it mildly, watching as the nurse entered on her rounds, pausing as she found Dougal watching her.

"He's awake? And alert?" The nurse hurried away, intent on calling Paul and alerting him, even though she knew that he would not be out of surgery for a couple of hours.

—

Dougal struggled to speak, his hand going to the ventilator mask, McKala's hand there to stop him. He wanted to rise from the bed but just didn't have the energy. He stared at the pieces of equipment surrounding him, puzzled as to what they were, why he was there, and just where he was. His eyes slid closed and he slept before he could determine just what was going on.

Abigayle had to persuade McKala to walk away, watching with compassion as McKala's head turned back to watch Dougal. Her reluctance to leave him was obvious. Dooley stood and watched her approach him, sharing a look with the two men standing beside him. Tag and Shay had shown up, hearing from Evan that Dougal had been hurt. Both men had been away with their wives when it had happened. Their appearance was not out of the ordinary, not for these friends, connected by a history that few could know about.

Dooley sent a questioning look at Abigayle, not seeing the woman who had perched herself near the door, her eyes intent on McKala, listening to their conversation.

"McKala?" Dooley's eyes raised once more to Abigayle when McKala didn't respond. "Abigayle?"

"Dougal was awake and alert. He's sleeping now." McKala moved away from them, stopping as she saw the woman before she marched towards her. "What are you doing here? You were told to stay away from me. Don't you get it?"

Dooley was beside her before she could finish speaking, a hand reaching to prevent the woman from disappearing.

"McKala? What is this all about?"

"She's been following me, all over the place. Watching me. Watching Camm and Cori. Do something." McKala spun on her heels and walked away, Tag beside her, Shay watching the woman closely.

"Is that a fact?" Dooley stared the woman down. "How be you come along with me and we'll have a chat about it?" He led her away, Shay following, watchful for anyone else.

Chapter 11

Duncan listened closely as Abigayle spoke, her voice low enough so that he was the only one who could hear her. Deveney had appeared as had Flannery, Ayron, and Breckon, drawing McKala and Cori away with them, to the outdoors. That was needed, McKala knew, but she was reluctant to do that. She was afraid for these new friends of hers, afraid that they would be hurt and it would be her fault. Camm was with Tag and Evan, somewhere around.

"What can we do, Duncan? She can't go on like this. Nor can Camm or Cori." Abigayle was distressed, that was easy to see.

"I know, love. Deveney is taken with the two of them. They think of her as an aunt figure."

Abigayle sighed once more. "But who is it that is after her? Do we have any idea?"

"Not yet. Dooley's spoken with me and even he has not much information. Whoever it is has kept themselves hidden. The woman that he arrested the other day has warrants out in other jurisdictions, he said, more serious that here and she has been transported away." To say Duncan was frustrated was an understatement. "Has Dougal been awake again?"

—

Abigayle shrugged. "Not when we've been in there. McKala wants you to go in next. You and Deveney."

"We will, love." Duncan searched the waiting room, not seeing either one of the young ladies. "Where are they? I thought that they would be back by now."

"They aren't, Duncan." Abigayle was on her feet, fear suddenly coursing through her body. "Where are they? Flannery, Ayron, and Breckon are back. Ladies, where are McKala and Deveney?"

Flannery looked up, shocked, before she was on her feet.

"They were right behind us. McKala stopped in the gift shop for a moment. She said they would be right up." Flannery almost ran for the stairs, Duncan on her heels as Abigayle and the other two ladies searched the floor that they were on, as best they could. Questions asked of the nurses brought negative responses.

Duncan flew down the steps, shoving the door at the bottom open with an almost violent gesture, startling those standing nearby. He searched the lobby and then the gift shop, not seeing them. He pulled out his phone, sending a text to Abigayle, who responded that they were not there. Had he found them?

Shay stood for a moment, watching before he walked towards Duncan, a hand out to stop him.

"Duncan? You're looking for someone?" Shay's voice held a tone that said he was afraid for McKala.

<hr>

"I am, Shay. Can you help?" Duncan ran his hands through his hair and then rubbed at his cheek. "I can't find McKala or Deveney. They didn't come back with the other ladies just a bit ago. They had stopped in the gift shop. I can't find them."

Shay stared at him for a moment before he pulled Duncan with him to the outside of the hospital.

"Explain to me what happened, Duncan."

"Your three wives, Deveney, McKala, and Cori had gone to the cafeteria. Everyone but Deveney and McKala came back. They had stopped in the gift shop for something, Flannery said. They never made it to the floor."

Shay nodded, his phone out to call it in.

"Breckon? Did they make it there?" Shay's eyes slid closed for a moment as his wife responded in the negative. "No, I'm with Duncan. I'm calling it in. We don't see them anywhere around here."

Brownie, an officer on the Lakeside police force and a friend of Shay's, approached, a frown momentarily on his face. He shook his head as he watched Duncan pace. *Not another one,* he prayed. *Please, Lord? Can we not catch a break of any kind?*

"Brownie?" Shay's hand was outstretched to shake Brownie's. "I didn't know that you were on duty today."

"I wasn't to be but was called in. What's happening?"

"You know about Dougal?"

"I heard that he had been shot. How is he?"

—

Shay shrugged. "I haven't heard today, but he's not wakening up like they expected him to." He turned to watch Duncan, seeing the older man just standing, a hand still on his cheek, devastation in his demeanour. "This is what's happening. The three wives and Duncan's daughter, McKala and Cori had gone for a meal. Deveney and McKala stopped at the gift shop. They never made it to the floor."

"They didn't? You've searched?" Brownie's eyes were searching, not seeing either of the ladies.

"Not yet. I stayed with Duncan. He said he has but he can't go everywhere in the hospital. That would be up to you and your fellow officers and security. And there's the head of security now."

Chapter 12

They had searched everywhere that they could, Brownie, his fellow officers, hospital security. The two ladies had not been found. Brownie searched the security feed, seeing McKala and Deveney heading into the gift shop but not coming out. He was on his feet, running for there, the head of the hospital security at his side.

Greg, the security head, stopped in the doorway to the gift shop, his keen eyes searching.

"They were here, Greg, but aren't now. I didn't see them leave." Brownie paced towards the counter and the only staff member on duty.

"No, they did. Amy, two young ladies came in here and never left. What do you know about that?"

Amy, in her early twenties, stared down her nose at the men, defiance in her stance.

"They did. I saw them leave." Amy turned away.

"Amy, that is not true." Greg looked around. "Has anyone else been in here?"

She shrugged. "It's a gift shop. People are in and out all the time."

Greg shared a look with Brownie before he headed for the door marked "Staff only".

—

"Hey, wait! You can't go in there! You're not staff!" Amy charged towards Greg, Brownie stepping into her way and stopping her. "Get out of my way! He can't go in there!"

"I can, Amy. And you well know it." Greg shared another look with Brownie, who nodded.

"How be you have a seat on your stool?" Brownie pointed behind her.

"I will not." Her belligerence came through loud and clear.

"I don't think you understand. This is not a request. This is a direct police directive. If you refuse, then I will arrest you for obstructing an officer."

"Like you can! This is hospital property. You can't do that." Amy refused to move away from Brownie, instead trying to pass him and head for where Greg was reaching to unlock the door.

Brownie sighed, reached for his handcuffs, and snapped them on Amy's wrists, despite her protests.

"You are now under arrest. Sit on that stool."

Brownie's hard look at her finally got through to Amy and she flopped down hard on her stool. She chewed at her lip. She had been promised good money to keep anyone out of the storeroom.

Greg's hand shoved open the now unlocked door, Brownie watching closely before he turned. Brownie pointed to Amy, asking the responding officers and security personnel to watch her and to not let her more. She was under arrest.

Greg stood for a moment, staring around the storeroom. To say it was a mess was an understatement. He had never seen it cluttered with boxes strewn around.

Brownie paused beside him before he shook his head.

"I gather it's not usually like this."

Greg sighed before he turned back to the door, beckoning a couple of officers to enter.

"No, it's usually nice and tidy. That makes me suspect that they were here and taken out that door." His finger stabbed at it. "Or else they are still here, waiting for the gift shop to close and then be taken out after dark."

Brownie began the process of stacking the boxes, spinning as he heard an exclamation from Greg. He was at his side, down on his knees.

"It's Deveney."

"Drugged, I suspect." Greg pointed to one of the officers. "Out the back door and find someone from Emerge to come in that way. This has to be kept as quiet as it can be." He watched as the officer nodded and then almost ran from the storeroom. "Now, where is McKala?"

"Here!"

Brownie was across the room, on his knees beside McKala, gently turning her over.

"Drugged as well, Greg." He looked around. "It's a crime scene now, fellows. We get the ladies out of here and then our force takes over."

—

Brownie stood to the side, watching as McKala and Deveney were assessed and then moved rapidly from the store room. His head shaking, he turned and walked back into the gift shop, stopping to watch Amy as she shifted on her stool, belligerence on her face. Turning to another office, he pointed to her and asked that she be taken to their detachment and interrogated.

Chapter 13

Duncan looked around as he heard his name called, his hand reaching for Abigayle's. Camm and Cori stood near them, fear on their faces. They had no idea where McKala was and they just needed her. Brownie approached them, a grim look on his face.

"Brownie?" Duncan was almost afraid to ask.

"We found them, Duncan. They're in the Emergency Department at the moment. I'll take you down but before we go, how is Dougal?"

"About the same." Abigayle shot a look over her shoulder. "He has not been awake, not since earlier. That's concerning everyone."

"I am sure that it is." He looked with compassion at Camm and Cori as they clung to one another. "How about it? Want to go and find McKala? She's sleeping right now."

"She is? Where was she?" Camm paced beside Brownie as he turned for the elevator, Cori's hand tight in his.

"She was in the gift shop, Camm, but not by choice. She and Deveney were sedated or drugged, we think. They have been awake but the doctors there want to keep them for a while, just to make sure that they're okay."

—

"McKala won't. She'll leave and come up to Dougal. That's what she'll do." Cori was adamant in her words, knowing her cousin only too well.

Duncan's arms were around the two youngsters, Abigayle's hand on his, as they approached the stretchers that the two young ladies were lying on. They could hear the sobs that Cori was trying hard to hide before her brother moved to hug her. They stood beside their cousin, hands on her arm, waiting for her to awaken.

Duncan and Abigayle watched Deveney, willing her to awake, turning as they heard footsteps. A physician stood there, charts in his hands, before he looked up.

"You're family?" He spoke quietly, a gentleness in his manner.

"Deveney is our daughter. McKala is guardian to these two." Duncan sighed, knowing that they would have questions that the physician not likely could answer. "How are they?"

"Sleeping right now. They have given their statements, but I am not sure how much of that they will remember. They were sedated. Any details of that and how they were found must come from the authorities."

"We understand, Doctor. When can we take them home?" Abigayle turned towards her daughter once more, suddenly afraid for her.

McKala roused later, listening carefully before her eyes opened. She glanced around, a breath of relief coming from her. They weren't captive any more. She slid from the stretcher, moving to stand beside Deveney before she crept to the door and then out, leaving the department and heading for the elevator.

Heading for Dougal, McKala didn't hear her name called or see Evan following her, a frown on his face as he did so. He stopped at the doorway to Dougal's room, watching carefully as she made her way to the bedside before he turned, his phone out to call someone. Only, Evan had no idea who to call.

McKala's hand rested against Dougal's face, seeing with relief that the ventilator was removed. She felt disoriented, not sure where he stood physically. A nurse appeared at her side, a hand out to brace McKala as she turned in fright.

"McKala? Are you okay? Should you be on your feet?"

"I need to be. I need to be here. Dougal needs me. Only I don't know how to help him." McKala blinked back the tears that threatened. "When can he leave the ICU?"

"Tomorrow, I think, McKala. He'll move to a regular room. The surgeon was looking for you earlier."

"Yeah, well, we know where I was, don't we?"

—

Chapter 14

Dougal shuffled slowly down the hallway of the medical floor, heading for the waiting room. He knew that his friends were there. His parents and sister had headed home, at his request. He didn't feel safe with them there, not when he had heard what happened to both Deveney and McKala. Dougal and McKala had talked about that very incident. McKala had not been able to give much information, other than they had been approached from behind, forced into the storeroom and then lost consciousness. How that was achieved, she wasn't quite sure, but she thought that she remembered a prick of a needle on her arm. The clerk, she adamantly stated, had been involved, locking the door and preventing them from leaving. The clerk, Amy, was just not talking.

McKala had tucked an arm around Dougal and his arm rested around her. She was afraid, she had to admit to herself, that he would never recover even though she was told that he would. Dougal nodded and then sank into the chair that she had manoeuvred him to, a deep breath taken to try and recover.

Evan stared at him before exchanging a glance with Tag and Shay. He didn't think that Dougal was that much better, but McKala had insisted that he was. He looked around, not seeing Camm and Cori.

"Where are Camm and Cori?"

"They went home with Dad and Mom." Dougal squinted at his friend. "We all thought it best." He shifted uneasily, discomfort in his chest driving that.

McKala watched him closely, seeing the discomfort that he was in and regretting that it was on her behalf. She felt his arm around her, drawing her close to him. She mentally shrugged. I'll allow it for now, she thought, but then things will change. I'll be out of his life shortly, and that I will regret. Please, Lord? Heal him. Protect me and the kids. Give me the strength and peace for when I move on and leave him. And that is something I am just not sure I can do, dear Lord.

Dooley watched for a moment before he approached and just sat, not saying anything. He grinned at McKala as she frowned at him. He saw her gaze go past him and remain that way. Dooley shifted in his seat, turning to stare the way that McKala was. He sighed. So much for visiting with a friend. His phone out, Dooley called Brownie, asking if he could send someone to the hospital. One of the men that they were searching for was there and intent on watching Dougal and McKala.

Late that evening, Dougal watched McKala as she paced his hospital room. He was due to be released the next day and he was glad. Glad that he could head home but not sure how McKala would take to his hometown of Cairn. He rose, deliberately stepping into her path and wrapping his arms around her.

"Talk to me, McKala. What has you so upset?" His arms wrapped around her.

McKala shrugged. "I just don't know, Dougal. I can feel something about to happen and I am not sure what. Does that even make sense?"

"It does." Dougal turned her towards the chair in the room, sinking down into it and then drawing her down on his knee, much to her surprise and then protest. "It's okay, my darlin'. You're fine. About that man in the waiting room today?"

"Him? He was one of the men. I'm scared that they will follow us to your home."

"Our home." Dougal corrected her without watching her face, not seeing the surprise and puzzlement on it. "We'll take what care we can, McKala. I won't be working for a while, so that will help."

"And just how would you be able to help take care of us? You're restricted in what you can do/"

"We'll figure it out. Now, about my home? You're okay with that?"

McKala shrugged, not quite sure what he was asking of her.

"I guess. Camm and Cori are taken with your town. They said someone named Ted had been around and was showing them the town and fun stuff to do."

"Ted? I thought that he would be. He's in his late teens, in college, but he's been a friend of mine for years. His father is the town doctor."

"He is? That's good then. You'll have someone to watch out for you." Her words were left unfinished, they both knew.

Chapter 15

The next day, McKala stood beside Dougal's truck, watching as he stared at the seat before she sighed. This was getting us nowhere, she thought. And there is someone out there watching us. I can feel them. I just can't see them. She turned as Evan and Flannery approached them.

"All set, McKala?" Evan was concerned to put it mildly. He had watched as she had looked around and knew what she was feeling. Both Flannery and he had had the same feelings when they went through what they did.

"I am. It's Dougal that seems to be having a problem." She smirked at Evan before she shook her head. "He needs help to get up on the seat and just won't ask for it. It's awkward when it's his left side that has to go on first."

"True. Unless he wants to ride in the back seat behind you. It would be easier getting in but I don't think that's what he wants." Evan moved forward, a hand out to help Dougal up and to the truck seat. "There you go, my friend. Listen. Flannery and I are going to follow you home and help you get settled." The two men shared a look before Dougal nodded, his strength depleted with the effort of just getting up into his truck.

—

"Thanks, Evan. Now, can we leave? I want to get McKala away from here." He stared around. "They're out there. I just don't know where."

"They are. And they will follow you. You can almost guarantee that they know who you are and where you live." Evan dipped his head to study McKala who had climbed behind the steering wheel.

"That's a given, Evan." Dougal watched carefully as McKala studied the truck and its instruments. "We're off, I guess. Thanks for following us."

Evan nodded before he headed for his own truck, seeing Shay and Tag waiting.

"You're on board?"

"We are, Evan. One of us will pull out in front of McKala, the other two behind her. I don't have a good feeling about this." Shay headed for his truck, intent on being in front.

"I agree." Tag spun in a circle. "There's more than one party involved, Evan. How do we ever find them?"

"That's a good question, Tag. I think we all asked a similar one. Unfortunately, it seems that they find us before we find them." Evan was frustrated that three of his friends had gone through or were now going through what he and Flannery had done. He hadn't wanted that at all. The only thing that he could do was to pray and pray hard.

Tag nodded, a thoughtful look on his face.

"How is Dougal, really?"

—

Evan shrugged. "He's trying hard to put up a good front and hide how he is feeling. Only that's not working so well. McKala has him pegged."

"She does at that." Tag waved and moved towards his truck, sliding in before he turned to Ayron. "All set, love?"

"I am. I just don't know that McKala is."

"I think you are right. McKala has learned to hide her emotions and her fears just to protect Camm and Cori. I would think it's been going on a lot longer than she will admit."

"I am sure it has. Now, what is the plan?"

"Shay is in front. Evan is right behind Dougal and then we follow. Just keep an eye out. We all need to stay safe. They would go after us to take us out if it meant that they could get to McKala."

"How sure are you all that it is just McKala?"

Tag shot Ayron a look and then nodded.

"Good point. Dougal could have someone after him. He's an officer. And then there was Holly and Lincoln and Logan and Aideen. Someone might want revenge for that."

"They could, but it seems far fetched."

"Not as far fetched as you would think. Okay, we're off. Pray for safety for us, love."

"I have been. I have such a horrible feeling." Ayron watched as the four vehicles pulled away from the parking lot, keeping close enough but not too close to one another. "Tag, McKala was muttering something earlier this morning about vengeance and an avenger. Do you have any idea what that is about?"

Tag thought for a moment before shaking his head.

"Not really, love. Unless she's thinking that God is our avenger and that vengeance is His."

"That could be. I don't know her well enough to judge where her faith is."

"She's struggling, Ayron, and has been for a while I would suspect. Being on the run like she was is hard enough if you're on your own. Pull in Camm and Cori and that just deepens her worry, fear and burden."

"It does. And now that she has Dougal in her life as well as all his friends, she's not sure where to turn or who to trust. I want to keep in touch with her. We're really not that far apart."

"Not really, forty-five minutes or so, depending on the weather and the traffic. Just short enough that we can do the trip weekly if it comes to that."

"And it will." Ayron stared out the window, her thoughts muddled before she began to petition God for protection for Dougal, McKala, Camm, and Cori. But she wasn't sure if her prayers would even help.

Chapter 16

McKala carefully backed the truck up into the driveway before she shoved the transmission into park and turned the ignition off. She stared around for a moment before her eyes centred on Dougal, seeing the whiteness of his face. He wasn't ready to come home yet, she thought. He needed a couple of more days but he just wouldn't do that. Dougal just had to come home. Now what, Lord? How do we do this?

Dougal roused, blinking to clear his vision before he reached for the door handle and then shoved the door open. He contemplated the drop to the ground and groaned. Somehow, today, a truck just wasn't the best vehicle for him to have. He looked up as Evan approached with a hand out to help him down.

Evan nodded at McKala, taking Dougal's keys and handing them to her.

"Open up for us, McKala. Dougal will take a while to get moving and into the house. We need to get you both out of sight as quickly as we can." He shared a glance with Tag and Shay who then moved to search the property.

Flannery, Ayron, and Breckon reached for the bags in the back seat before heading after McKala, sympathy on their faces at the look on her own face. McKala just wasn't sure about this, entering Dougal's house, even though as his bride it was her home. It just felt too strange. *Lord,* she prayed, *we need You to be here, to help us through the next while. Please heal Dougal.*

Entering the sprawling bungalow, McKala paused, her eyes closing, feeling as if she had just come home. And she had. Only she wasn't sure that was where God wanted her. An arm around her had her jumping for a moment before she heard Flannery's prayer just for her. Flannery understood to some degree how McKala felt, not having had a home for years before she had married Evan.

Later that afternoon, McKala wandered the house, trying to imagine living there for the rest of her life but just not able to. She just knew that she and Dougal would go their separate ways. Duncan and Abigayle were due in shortly, she knew, bringing Camm and Cori with them. She was anxious, she knew, just needing to see her cousins and ensure that they were indeed all right, even though they had both assured her that they were. They had explored the town with Ted and Holly and loved it, they said. They didn't want to leave it, ever.

She paused in the living room, her eyes on Dougal. He had stretched out on the couch a couple of hours ago and drifted off to sleep. She dropped to a sitting position beside him, a hand resting on his arm for a moment. *I don't get it, Lord. Why Dougal? How did he just happen to be there? And how did Cori know that he was the one to ask for help? Heal him, dear Lord. Let him feel that touch of the garment.*

McKala drifted off to sleep, the strain of the last two weeks taking its toll on her. She didn't know that Dougal had roused as she touched his hand, his eyes on her. Dougal raised himself to a sitting position, waiting for the pain to diminished before he roused McKala enough to have her move to sit beside him. McKala was asleep again, not feeling Dougal's arm around her to draw her close to him and didn't see his head tilt to watch her face. The kiss that he dropped on her forehead went unnoticed, except that McKala felt it in her heart and that helped with the healing that she was doing.

Dougal watched her for a moment before his head dropped back and he stared at the ceiling. *Lord, I love this lady. She's my helpmeet, my Proverbs 31 lady, the one that You destined before time began to be mine. How do we do this? She will walk on me when this adventure that we are in is all resolved. I don't want that. I don't want to lose her but I have to set her free. I know that. Only, Lord, I don't want to. Please protect us, solve this, and help us to decide just what we do want.*

Chapter 17

Neither one of the young couple heard the tap at the back door or the sounds of it opening and then quiet movement as Duncan, Abigayle, and the two youngsters entering the kitchen. Camm and Cori had been through the house with Duncan and Abigayle a couple of days before, exploring their new living quarters, excited at being in a house and not an apartment as they had been for so long.

Duncan set the box containing their dinner on the counter before Abigayle reached for the crockpot and plugged it in, keeping the meal warm. Cori was tight to her, asking what she could do to help. Camm and Cori had taken to the older couple, thinking of them as relatives, not having had grandparents in their lives for many years. They couldn't remember either set.

Standing in the hallway, Duncan watched as the younger couple still slept, concerned that they had not heard the noise of their entrance. He felt Abigayle's hand on his arm.

"They didn't wake up?" Her voice was quiet as she spoke.

"No, and that's concerning. It could have been anyone." Duncan sighed, knowing that his son and his bride were at their limit or even past it. "How do we keep them safe? Dougal's supervisor said he would be around tomorrow, but that he doesn't expect

—

Dougal to be back to work any time soon." He turned as he heard Camm's voice, rapidly moving towards him, hearing the sound of fear in Camm's voice.

"Duncan? What's this?" Camm stood just outside the kitchen door, his eyes on the back deck.

"What's what?" Duncan stood beside him, an arm around the young man's shoulders.

"That!" Camm pointed at the package that sat there. "What is that? It wasn't here the other day when we were through. Cori and I spent a lot of time out here and it wasn't there."

Duncan studied the box and then lifted his eyes to look around. He didn't see anyone but he was sure that the box had not been there when they had stepped up on the porch.

"Inside, Camm. We need to call it in. This is not what they need right now." Duncan shook his head at Abigayle as he pulled out his phone. "Have either one awakened yet?"

"Dougal was stirring. McKala is still sleeping. She didn't sleep much in the last couple of weeks." Abigayle moved to stand and watch the younger couple. "She told me that she was afraid to. That Dougal would die on her if she did sleep."

Cori hugged Abigayle.

"Did she say that? She used to say that to us. That one of us would disappear on her if she slept."

Camm nodded. "She was bad for that the last few months since we were on the run. She would only sleep for a couple of hours at a time. I would wake up and find her watching. She just couldn't tell me who she was watching for."

The older couple could hear the fear in the youngsters' voices and exchanged a look. How did they solve this, they asked themselves, and not bring harm to anyone else?

Dougal roused at last, blinking as he looked around. He stared down at McKala, not remembering that he had raised her to sit beside him. All he knew was that she was where she should be. He didn't want to lose her and feared that very thing. Looking up as he heard footsteps, Dougal sighed. James was here and in his uniform. That was not good, he thought.

"Dougal?" James' voice held a question.

"Yeah, I'm awake. Why are you here?"

"Your dad called. There was a package on the back porch. Interesting material in it."

"They're starting that, are they?" Dougal's head went back as his eyes closed. He drew in a deep breath. "How bad?"

"Bad enough. Pictures of you in the hospital. Of McKala there as well. A note that threatened you with death. Only we have no idea why."

"No, we never do, do we? And I have no idea why other than I walked in and helped her." Dougal raised his head, his eyes on the doorway. He could hear his parents' voices and those of Camm and Cori. "Did they threaten Camm and Cori?"

———

"No, that they have not done." James looked up from his notebook. "What are your thoughts, Dougal?"

Dougal shrugged, puzzled as to what was happening.

"I have no idea, James. McKala and I have not had a chance to talk. I was too worried about her and making sure that she was safe to even begin to go there with her. I should have. Only she wouldn't have talked. Whenever I tried to, she walked away from me." Dougal's eyes were on McKala, not seeing the speculative glance that James sent his way.

Chapter 18

McKala listened to Dougal talking with another man, someone who she didn't know. It has to be an officer, she thought, her head raising as she heard what they were saying. A package? Of course, there would be. That's what they always did. McKala had known that they were being watched in the hospital. Dooley had taken away the one woman, but she had felt the eyes of others on her, following her wherever she went.

Dougal's attention went to McKala, his heart hurting for his lady. This should not be happening, Lord. He sighed to himself, something he thought he had been doing a lot of lately. He wanted to protect her but couldn't. Not at the present time. And McKala should not have had to make a decision to marry, just to keep herself and her cousins safe. She had lost out on falling in love, going through the courtship, and then the wedding.

"McKala?"

Dougal's voice brought her eyes to him. She frowned as she watched his face.

"Dougal? You said there were photos?"

"There are, darlin'. Of both of us. Not of Camm and Cori nor my family or friends."

"No, they don't do that at first. But they will." McKala stared at James. "And who is this?"

“This is a fellow officer, McKala. James Wight. He’s the one who responded to the call.” Dougal’s arm tightened around her. “He may have questions to ask you.”

“He can ask but I am not sure that I have the answers.” McKala was on her feet, moving away from the two men. She left Dougal staring after her, consternation on his face.

“Did she really just do that?” Dougal made a motion to rise, staying still as James shook his head.

“She’s running, Dougal. She’s afraid for herself and everyone around her. McKala will try to come up with a way to keep everyone safe.” James shot a look behind him towards the kitchen. “She’s been on her own now for years, without someone that she can depend on to help her. McKala’s not sure who that is. She thinks it’s you but she doesn’t know you well enough to be sure. That trust will be hard for her to develop.”

“I know. And I can’t do it for her. Develop that trust, I mean. Only God can. Right now, I’m not sure how her faith is.” Dougal stared at the hands that he was rubbing together. “I want this over, James.”

“We know that you do. If we could end it today, we would.” James stood, watching Dougal closely. “How long are you off work for?”

“The surgeon didn’t say. Just told me to follow up with Doc.” Dougal sighed, knowing that he might never be able to return to the work that he loved. “I really don’t know, James.” He was on his feet, following James to the door. “You’ll keep me updated? Or rather us? I can't leave McKala out of this."

"We know you can't." James hesitated, not quite sure how to phrase his next words. "Don't go out there looking for vengeance, Dougal. That never works."

"I know. I want to do that, to avenge McKala and the youngsters. But it's not my place. It's God's."

Dougal stood for a moment on his front porch, just staring around the yard. Ted had been around, he could tell, doing the lawn maintenance. He would need to track him down and thank him, he thought. He felt a hand on his arm and simply reached to wrap it around McKala. McKala looked up at him, a frown on her face, not quite sure what he was up to. But she decided that she could grow to like this and that just wouldn't do. She was too dangerous. Only, she didn't know why or who.

"Dougal? Should you be up?"

"I need to move around, darlin'. That is what I was told." Dougal smiled at her before he turned them back into the house. "Now, Mom and Dad are here. Mom brought a meal?"

"She did. We're ready to eat if you are."

Neither saw the man standing on the sidewalk, in plain view, staring at the closing door. He looked around and then walked rapidly away, anger in his steps.

———

Chapter 19

McKala wandered the aisles at the local grocery store, not sure on what she should actually be buying. Dougal had simply handed her money, told her where to shop, and that he would not tell her what to buy. He had grinned at her as she had protested.

James watched her closely, before his eyes lifted. He was in there after his shift, still in his uniform. He hesitated to approach her. Instead, he monitored those around her, seeing the smiles that were directed her way. McKala tentatively smiled back at the people before she moved on to pay for the groceries and then head for the truck.

Stuffing the bags into the back seat, she turned to head back with her cart, stopping as she saw the men watching her. She moved away from the truck, leaving the cart outside the store before she headed to the pharmacy next door.

Hearing a scream for help, James spun from where he had parked and then ran for Dougal's truck. He could see McKala struggling against the arms that were wrapped around her. He slid to a halt, his weapon out and pointed at the two men.

"Let her go!" His voice barked at them, surprising them.

"Not a chance! She goes with us!" The man who held McKala tried to inch away, stopping as he felt something poke him in the back. They had not seen other officers in the area who had responded and now surrounded them.

"Let her go!" James waited before he moved closer, a hand out to grasp the man's wrist and drag it behind him. "McKala! Now! To my car. Edward?"

Edward, a fellow officer, ran with McKala to the police vehicles, stopping as she dug in her heels.

"No, I can't leave Dougal's truck!" She tried her best to get back there.

"No, you can't go back there. It's McKala?" At her nod, he simply shoved her into the car and then stood, his back to the door, and watched the commotion.

James finally walked towards Edward, a stern look on his face. His eyes sought McKala's, finding her watching him, fear on her face, but also a look that he just couldn't read.

"The paramedics have been around?"

Edward nodded.

"They have. She has some bruising on her arms and on her face." Edward stared towards Dougal's truck, now a crime scene. "How do we tell Dougal?"

"We won't. McKala will." James slumped against the car. "This wasn't supposed to happen, you know. She was just in getting groceries that are now in the back of the truck. Any chance that we can get them out?"

———

Edward nodded, heading that way. He knew what James didn't say. That Dougal's truck would not be leaving there any time soon.

James watched as McKala shoved open the door and then moved to walk towards the truck. His hand on her arm stopped her.

"It's a crime scene, McKala. Edward will retrieve your groceries and one of us will give you a ride home. Just let me have the keys and we'll get the truck to you."

McKala sighed. Today had not been a good day. She hated shopping to begin with and now this? To top it off, it was the anniversary of her aunt and uncle's deaths. She needed to be with Camm and Cori. And right now? That was not happening.

"Okay. Here." She dropped the keys into his hands. "How soon?"

"How soon?" James wasn't quite sure what she meant. He didn't often feel confused or bereft of knowledge about a victim. With McKala, however, that was exactly how he felt.

"Yes. How soon can I go home? Or to Dougal's. I don't think it's my home." McKala's face held a sadness that disturbed James. "It's just not this, James. Today has not been a good day." She blinked rapidly to dispel the tears. "It's that today is the day that I lost my aunt and uncle and became guardian to Camm and Cori. I need to get back to them."

James nodded, reaching for the bags of groceries, before he pointed with a full hand towards his vehicle.

"Over there, McKala. Let me drive you home. You've given your statement?"

McKala nodded.

"I did. It seems that all I do is give statements lately. I'm tired of it. When does it end, James? When Dougal's dead?"

Chapter 20

His eyes on McKala as she moved around the kitchen putting away the groceries, Dougal listened to James' quiet words. His eyes slid shut as to how close it was to McKala disappearing. That was the plan, he had no doubt.

"Did she say anything about them?" Dougal's voice was equally quiet. He just wasn't sure how to respond to McKala, at least not yet.

"Not really. Other than it was an anniversary of the youngsters losing their parents. She was young when she took them on."

"She was. Too young. She hasn't had a chance to be a young adult." Dougal sighed. "And then we married as we did."

"You felt that you had no choice. I know you, Dougal. You would not have taken this step if there had been any other." James watched Dougal carefully before he nodded. He's in love with McKala, not sure how she feels, and is reluctant to tell her his feelings, James thought. What a quagmire to be in!

"Edward will drop off the truck?" Dougal turned towards James for a moment.

"He will. I'm not sure when. He's on duty to around eleven, he said. I'm on my way home. If you need me, call me." James approached McKala,

—

waiting until she turned to him. "McKala, call me if you need me or one of the other officers. You're family." He waited for her to react. When she didn't and just watched him, he nodded and walked away, his thoughts muddled at the present time. How do we help them?

Dougal turned back from the door after watching James leave, having searched the area. He could feel them out there, whoever it was. He would need to look around the house, that he was sure of, and soon. No doubt, they had tried to enter and failed. But who knew what they had left on the outside. He was suddenly afraid for his family.

Standing near the counter in the kitchen, Dougal studied McKala carefully, not sure how to approach her. He knew that he loved this lady, had since he laid eyes on her, but was just not sure how to tell her that. And that was unusual for him. He wasn't usually at a loss for words.

"McKala? What happened today?"

McKala paused in her movements, not sure how to respond or even what Dougal was asking.

"What do you mean?" She refused to turn and look at him.

"Today? What happened? Something did. James told me what he saw. But I need you to talk to me."

McKala spun, anger sparking from her.

"And say what? That someone tried to abduct me, take me, whatever you want to call it? In broad daylight? And from a busy store parking lot?" She shook in her fear. "If James hadn't been there and heard me scream, we wouldn't be having this conversation. I saw the people. They wouldn't help."

"Oh, McKala!" Dougal reached for her, finding her backing away from him. "They would have."

"No, they were moving away. No one called for help. Is this the kind of town that I came to? Maybe I should just take Camm and Cori and leave."

"No, don't. You'd take my heart with you." Dougal didn't understand that he had just put it all on the line with McKala. "They would have. I know they would. They know that you are my wife. Word has gotten around. They look out for families here."

"Well, yeah, maybe. I didn't see that happening." McKala spun away from him, heading for the pantry, and pulling out pasta for a meal, thumping the package down on the countertop.

Dougal winced at that, hoping that she hadn't broken the pasta. She just might have, he thought. He moved back into her space, trapping her by the counter before he reached to draw her into his hug.

"I know it's a bad day. Camm talked to me this morning." His head rested against hers. "What can I do to help? And I am working on finding whoever it is."

McKala finally nodded, her hair brushing against his chin.

"I know, but I am just so scared for Camm and Cori. I can't handle it if something happens to them. It's just a bad day."

"I know, darlin'. I know. But what can I do for you?"

McKala shrugged. "Find who this is." She leaned back to look at him, taking in his white face and the dark shadows under his eyes. "Dougal, you need to lie down. You're almost out on your feet."

"Not while you need me." He turned them to head for the living room, dropping down on the couch with a groan. "Now, talk to me, McKala. Where do we go from here with what we need to find out?"

Chapter 21

An hour later, McKala stared down at the bag of pasta that she had thumped down on the countertop. No, she thought, this is not what I wanted to make for supper. At the present time, I am not really interested in making anything and I have to. She turned her head as she heard Dougal's step, shuffling this time, and spun to watch him. No, McKala thought, he isn't doing well at all. I need to find the number for that doctor friend of his.

Dougal paused as he entered the kitchen, a hand out on the back of a chair. He was finding it more difficult to breathe as the day went by and just couldn't understand it. He raised his eyes to find McKala watching him before they closed and he collapsed to the floor. Dougal didn't hear McKala's scream before she was at his side, hands trying to roll him over and not succeeding. She was on her feet, heading for her phone, dialling 911 before she dropped her phone and was back on her knees, tears on her face.

"Dougal? Please! Dougal, I need you to wake up!" McKala rolled him to his back, her hands reaching to check for a pulse. She breathed a little easier, finding one, before she was on her feet, hearing a noise at the door.

The paramedics paused at the open door, exchanging a look with one another before they

85

headed in. The stretcher rumbled as they pulled it with them before one exclaimed and then was on his own knees beside Dougal. A stethoscope was out as Dan listened for a heart beat. He shook his head at his partner, Eva.

"Dougal's alive, Eva. But he can hardly breathe. Why?"

"Duncan told me that Dougal had been shot and it just missed the heart. I wonder." Her hands were on his leg, turning it. "There. Heat and swelling. A blood clot likely."

Dan paled and then nodded. "Call it in, Eva. We'll need to move and move quickly." He looked around. "Dispatch said a McKala called it in. Where is she?"

Eva was on her feet, searching.

"She's not here. I don't like that, Dan."

Dan shook his head and then reached to help lift Dougal to the stretcher, turning as he heard footsteps.

"Dan? What do you have?" James stood there, the sunlight glinting off his badge.

"Dougal's down. Not sure why. But McKala, is it?" When James nodded, Dan and Eva exchanged a glance. "She called it in. She's nowhere around."

James paused, his eyes on Dan.

"She's not? I don't like that. Head off with Dougal. Someone will head for Duncan."

James stood and watched as they left before he began his own search, pausing at the front door. Signs of a struggle stared him in the face. He sighed.

———

This is not what he wanted to find. McKala had disappeared. The question was who had her.

Duncan almost ran for the clerk as he cleared the doors to the Emergency Room.

"Sally? Dougal?"

Sally looked up, compassion on her face.

"The docs are with him. I'll let them know you are here." She went to rise, pausing as Duncan raised a hand.

"McKala? Is she here?"

"McKala? I'm not sure who you mean."

"McKala. Dougal's wife. Is she here?"

Sally shook her head.

"He was on his own, Dougal, as far as I know. Let me find Doc for you. He's working today."

Duncan paced. His ladies, as he termed them, had headed out of town with Camm and Cori and were not due back until late, that he knew. He sighed, knowing that he would need to call them and ask them to come back soon.

Doc paused in his rushed examination of Dougal, nodding at Sally's words.

"McKala wasn't there? I don't like that, Sally. Talk to an officer. Find out if it has been reported." He turned back when he finished, his assessment a priority.

Sally stared at him and then shrugged, finding her way to Duncan.

—

"She's not here, Duncan. Sorry."

Sally was almost flippant in her remarks. Duncan frowned at her as she turned away and headed back to her desk. Sally had wanted to be the one Dougal spent his life with. Only he had never noticed her. To hear that he was married? That angered her. She would find some way to avenge that and then draw Dougal to herself.

Chapter 22

Her heart stuttering for a moment in her terror for her son, Abigayle listened to Duncan.

"Duncan? What aren't you saying?" She turned as she heard Deveney, Camm, and Cori approaching her, laughter wafting ahead of them. It distressed Abigayle that she had to cut their day short. It had been fun, she had decided earlier. It had been a long time since she had spent a day with youngsters that age.

"Mom?" Deveney paused, seeing the look of fear and worry on her mother's face.

"Dad called. We need to head home and now. I'll explain as we go."

Deveney stared at her mother as she pulled away from the downtown area of Holly. She knew they had at least an hour's drive to get home.

"What did Dad say?"

Abigayle drew in a deep, shuddering breath.

"Dougal collapsed a couple of hours ago. He's being assessed in the hospital. Doc's on duty."

Deveney looked at the youngsters, seeing the fear and worry on their faces.

"Did he say why?"

—

"Not for sure, but Doc was doing an ultrasound. He thinks a blood clot."

"A blood clot?" Deveney's voice rose. "No! Not that!"

"What has McKala said?" Cori's worried little voice wafted to the front seat.

"That's the thing, Cori. McKala wasn't there. She called 911. They didn't see her." Abigayle shared a look with her daughter, who began to pray audibly.

Camm stared out the window, watching as a police cruiser sped past them and then pulled in front of them, leading them it seemed.

"What's he doing? Abigayle, why is he staying just ahead of us?"

Abigayle drew in a deep breath even as her foot pressed the pedal to catch up with him.

"God sent him, Camm. He's escorting us to Dougal. Someone must have called him."

"James would." Deveney didn't say anything, but she and James had been dating.

James turned as he heard his name called and sighed to himself. Just what he needed, wasn't it? He walked towards his sergeant, not sure why the man was there.

"James? What can you tell me?" Ted Sharpe looked past him at the house.

"Dougal collapsed. He's being assessed right now from what I'm told. McKala is the one who called it in. But she is nowhere around. Her purse is there. The techs say there looks like there was a struggle near the front door. I have to agree with them." James squinted at the sun. "It's getting late, Ted. Where is she?"

"That we have to determine. Any thoughts?" Ted watched him closely.

James shrugged.

"I don't have a lot. I know that she was on the run for months with her cousins. Dougal stepped in to help."

"I understand that. Where are the kids?"

"With Abigayle and Deveney. They were heading to Holly, just to give them something fun to do and to help pass the time for them." James sighed once more. "Deveney sent me a text earlier today. She thought that they were being followed. I asked for her to let me know once they were heading home and I'd make sure that they had an escort."

James' attention went to the garage door and he strode rapidly that way, Ted on his heels.

"Where did this come from?" James looked around. "It wasn't here earlier. I know that. Who put it here?"

"Dougal's security camera?"

"It's been disabled, likely when they took McKala." James was frustrated. A friend and fellow officer was suffering, his wife was missing, and they had no idea where to look or even who to look for.

Ted beckoned for a crime scene tech.

—

"Work on that, please, Sally? Let us know what you find out about it." He turned to James. "Have you had any word on Dougal?"

James shook his head.

"Not yet. Duncan said he'd call but he was told that Dougal was in critical condition."

Chapter 23

Duncan turned as he heard footsteps approaching him and then paused, noting the grave look on the physician's face.

"David?"

"Duncan? You can come back. Abigayle isn't here?"

"No, she and Deveney had taken Camm and Cori to Holly today. And McKala, Dougal's wife, is missing."

"His wife? I don't know that we had her down as a next of kin."

"We need to change that. Even though she isn't here, she is his next of kin." Duncan rubbed at his face, fatigue hitting in waves. "What can you tell me?"

David Taylor frowned as he watched the younger woman edging closer to where they stood. She seemed intent on listening in on what they were speaking out. David's hand on Duncan's arm drew him back towards where Dougal lay.

"This way, Duncan. You can see him for a while, but be warned. He is in critical condition. At this point, we don't know if he will recover."

Duncan nodded soberly, his eyes on his son.

"What happened, David?"

—

93

"He had surgery, what about two to three weeks ago?" At Duncan's nod, David sighed. This was always so hard. "He developed a blood clot in his leg. He may not have known it or simply ignored the symptoms."

"I can see him doing just that, David. He was that worried about McKala. He was shot by the men trying to abduct McKala. Only it seems that they succeeded."

"Okay. That can explain it. Part of the clot broke off and made its way to his lung. That is what we call a pulmonary embolism. It is life threatening, as you are aware. As of now, we have done what imaging we need. He is on a blood thinner and also a clot buster." Daniel studied his friend and fellow church member. "He will be in the ICU for now."

Duncan nodded as his feet took him towards his son. Why, Lord? He couldn't express his thoughts any better than that, but he knew that God had heard. It was just that they might not like the answers that they received.

Studying his son, he sighed. *This was not to have happened,* he thought. *We need Dougal well and on his feet. He will be devastated to learn that McKala has gone missing. How do we ever explain that to him? And how do we explain that to the youngsters?* He stepped back as the nurses came to move Dougal to another floor, to another unit. A unit that no one knew for sure that he would ever live to come out of, Duncan thought.

Heading for the waiting room, Duncan paused before he turned, hearing rushing footsteps approaching him. He simply wrapped Abigayle in his arms, his eyes on the young woman that David had watched. He frowned. No, he didn't know her, but she seemed too interested in what was happening with them.

"Duncan? What news?" Abigayle stepped back as Duncan reached for his daughter and then Camm and Cori.

"It's a blood clot in his lung. He's on medications for that but he is critical, love. They've moved him to the ICU. Let's head that way."

"But Dad? Where's McKala?" Deveney searched for her sister-in-law, not seeing her. "Is she already up there?"

Duncan sighed once more as he shepherded his family onto the elevator, watching as the door shut in the younger woman's face. He would need to speak with James or someone, he thought. She was just too intent on finding out what was going on.

"I'm sorry, Deveney. Camm, Cori? McKala disappeared just after she called for help for Dougal. We don't know where she is at present." His arms came out to gather the two close to him. "We're looking, I can guarantee you that."

"He got her!" Camm's angry voice echoed in the elevator even as the doors slid open and they walked off, heading for the nursing station. "Can't he leave us alone?"

"Who took her? Camm? Do you know?"

Camm nodded. "I saw him once watching McKala. I took a picture of him. I'm sorry,

Duncan." Tears filled the young man's eyes as a sober look settled on his face. "I should have remembered. And it's my fault."

"Never your fault, Camm. You likely didn't think it was important. We have all been there." Deveney's arm came around Camm and then her other arm drew Cori to her. "We'll find James and send it to him. It's on your phone?"

Camm nodded, his hand reaching out with his phone, the picture drawn up.

"This is him. Can we send it to James now?" He was almost pleading with the lady he now considered an aunt.

"We can." Deveney reached for the phone, studied the man, and then sent the picture to James and then to her own phone. "There. James will get it shortly. He'll talk to you, Camm, about this."

James pulled out his phone as it chimed, a frown on his face as he saw the message was from Camm. This is odd, he thought, even as he opened the message. His hand froze as it hovered over the message and then he looked at the photo. Not who he wanted to see, James thought, turning to look for Ted.

"Ted?" James almost ran towards him. "Camm just sent me this. He told Duncan that he had a picture he had forgotten about. Deveney sent it on. Camm told them he found the man watching McKala. I know who is after her. Or least one of his henchmen."

Ted studied his officer before he took James' phone. He drew in a sharp breath as he saw the photo.

—

96

"Him? We need to find her and fast, James."

"Only we have no idea where he has her." James spun in a circle. "Someone is watching us."

"That they are. Sally opened the envelope. It's a demand for McKala to provide photos and documents to someone else."

"There are two parties after her? I don't like that." James drew in a deep breath, knowing that their work had just doubled. And he had no idea yet on where to take it. He had to leave it for the detectives, he thought, but he knew that he would be investigating as well. James didn't have it in him to leave it alone. Not when it was a friend and his wife.

Chapter 24

Evan, Tag, Shay, and Dooley, a friend of Evan's and an officer on the force in his town, walked shoulder to shoulder across the high school football field in Dougal's town. The three ladies, Flannery, Ayron, and Breckon, were with Dougal's family in the ICU waiting room. Shay had been awake all night, reaching for his phone before dawn had even broken through the eastern sky. He was adamant that they needed to search near the football field. God had kept him awake all night in prayer and had impressed on him that was where they needed to search and search as early that morning as they could.

"How sure are you about this, Shay?" Evan expressed the thoughts of the other three.

Shay shrugged. "I'm not real sure in any way that we can prove. It's more that God spoke to me and told me we had to search here. That He would lead us to McKala." Shay studied the sky and then the football field. "I just had to follow that, guys. It's like when I was undercover. If I had a real sense of God leading, I followed it. That kept me alive more times than I know about."

The four men exchanged glances. They all knew what Shay meant. God had done that with them all at some point.

"Is James around?" Tag turned backwards to look behind them.

—

"He's in court today, until noon anyway. He said he'd call." Evan reached for his phone and studied the message. "Flannery just sent a text. No change with Dougal. They're trying everything but nothing seems to be working."

"It's like he knows McKala is missing. He's grieving." Shay nodded.

"He's giving up, is what is not being said." Dooley sighed. "Is nothing easy with you guys?"

The three men with him laughed before they stopped walking. A short conversation had them splitting into pairs. Tag and Dooley walked one way, Evan and Shay the other.

"Do you think we'll find her, Evan?" Shay was worried that he had brought them out on a wild goose chase.

"You are convinced that we will. God had given you that confidence. We both know that He doesn't do that unless it is what will happen." Evan paused, his eyes searching along the debris scattered along the fence. "I can see them dumping her, if not here, then somewhere. She didn't strike me as the type of person that would cave under pressure."

"I don't know her as well as you do, but that's my impression of her. She looks fragile but she has steel running through her." Shay's voice stopped, and then he was running for the fence, to drop to his knees.

Evan stared at him before he was running after him, crouching down, a hand gripping the chain-link fence as he stared down at the body in front of him. A woman, he thought.

—

Shay's knees had nudged to body gently as he dropped to them, a hand reaching for the lady's back. A sigh of relief escaped him as he felt the slow rise and fall of her back. He was afraid, though, as the breathing was shallow and laboured. Shay leaned forward, unable to see the lady's face for the arm across her head. He heard Evan draw in a deep breath.

"It's McKala, Shay. I recognize her engagement ring. It is so unique." Evan was on his feet, heading for Tag and Dooley. "It's her, fellows. Let's get help for her." He shrugged out of his jacket even as he turned back to her, dropping it on her to try and help warm her. "Shay?"

"She's alive, Evan. I just don't know how hurt she is." Shay looked up, squinting against the sun. "You called it in?"

"I did." Evan looked around, as they heard the sirens rising and falling as they approached and then cut off. The red and blue of the emergency lights flashed around the scene even as the vehicles emptied and men and women ran their way. "That didn't take long for help to arrive."

James ran towards them, his tie flapping in the wind as he did so. He had just left the courtroom, the case he had been to testify in resolved without going to trial, when he heard the call come in.

"Evan? You have news?" James slid to a stop, his eyes searching the men's faces before they dropped to the ground. He was on his knees beside Shay, not caring that the dampness of the early morning dew soaked through his dress trousers.

"It's McKala, James. God told me we needed to search here and today, as early as we could." Shay was on his feet, his hands reaching for Evan's jacket as it was removed so that the paramedics could work on her.

"God has indeed led you." James stood for a moment, a thoughtful look on his face. "We'll need your statements and then you can head into the hospital." He looked around as Ted stopped beside him. "It's McKala."

"I see. You're with her, James, no matter where she goes. I'll head in shortly."

Chapter 25

Duncan looked around as he heard footsteps heading his way, on his feet as he watched the three younger men walking towards him. Dooley had taken off to head home, having to go on duty that afternoon. Frowning, Duncan hesitated to approach them, not sure why they were there. Deveney had taken the two youngsters home and Abigayle was with Dougal. The three ladies watched carefully as their fellows approached, reading them correctly that they had news for Duncan.

"Fellows? I don't think this is just a casual visit, is it?" He searched their faces, seeing something that gave him hope. "McKala?"

"We have her, Duncan." Shay spoke even as Evan's hand went out to steady Duncan. "We found her a bit ago. She's downstairs right now in Emergency."

"You found her?" Duncan stared at the three men before he sank back into his chair. "You've found her. Praise God!" He peered at them through tears eyes. "Is she hurt?"

"We don't know, Duncan." Evan crouched down in front of him. "We found her and then let the emergency people move in. I'm told that you and Abigayle are her next of kin, after Dougal."

———

"We are." Duncan was torn, wanting to stay near Dougal but knowing that his son would want him with McKala. "Let's head down."

"Where's Abigayle and the rest?" Tag looked around for his friends.

"Abigayle is with Dougal. Deveney took the youngsters home late last night. They are due back in soon." Duncan hesitated, wanting to wait for them, but driven to find out how McKala was.

"Our ladies will watch for them." Evan's arm was around Duncan's shoulders as he prayed for his friend and his family. "We'll get you downstairs to McKala and then sort out everything else as we can. James said he would be by later."

"James? Was he there? I thought he had to be in court." Duncan moved slowly towards the elevator, his emotions in a mess.

"He was. His court case was cancelled." Shay studied the older man, seeing how he was fighting to control his emotions and not succeeding very well.

Duncan stood for a moment, staring at the physician, someone that he didn't know before he walked to the stretcher. He studied McKala, not sure what the physician had meant.

"I'm sorry, Doctor. I thought you said that she wasn't speaking."

The man sighed. "That's exactly what I said. She has not responded verbally to any questions or comments at all. She is awake or was rather. I would like to keep her in overnight, just to rehydrate her and repeat the blood work in the morning. I understand that her husband is not available to sign any consents." They could hear the contempt and disgust in the man's voice.

"I want another physician to take over her care." Duncan's hand went up as the man went to protest. "No, this is my town. I will have another physician take over her care." He stared the physician down. "Just so you know? My son is not here and it's not because he would not wish to be. He was shot about two weeks ago when someone tried to abduct McKala. He collapsed three days ago from an embolism and is in the ICU right now. Perhaps you need to find out the information you should have before you start making judgment calls. Now, who is taking over her care?"

Early the next morning, McKala stood beside Dougal, a hand on his, her other arm wrapping around herself. She had just stared at the nurse before she had scrambled from her bed and rushed to dress, not heeding the words that she couldn't do that.

McKala had found the ICU and then crept in to stand near Dougal. She hated that he had been hurt because of her and was even now in danger. Duncan and Abigayle had been around yesterday, was it only a day ago? Deveney had brought in Camm and Cori, who had stared at their cousin, unsure as to why she wasn't speaking.

She blinked rapidly, not willing to let the tears fall. She had cried enough, she thought, enough for a lifetime. McKala wanted this over with but was really not sure how to do that. The man who had taken her had demanded photos, documents, financial information from her, information that she didn't have and had no idea why he was asking her for it. The threats that he had levelled at her had terrified her. McKala's voice had frozen, leaving her too terrified to speak. She had been unable to avoid the blow that had sent her spinning into a brick wall and then to the dirt floor. The man had stood over the fallen McKala, rage building in him that she was not responding to his demands and threats. He had stared around and then lifted her to throw over his shoulder. McKala's body had been dumped in the the football field, during the night, no one around to question the man or come to her aid.

Chapter 26

A week later, Dougal was on his feet and at home, shrugging off the concerns and worry of his family and friends. His whole focus was McKala. He was puzzled that she didn't, or was it, wouldn't speak. Dougal had tried his utmost to make her. McKala had looked at him, a shuttered blank look on her face and then just walked away, leaving him to stand and stare after her, a hand rubbing at his face.

McKala knew that Dougal wanted, no needed to know what had happened to her. She just couldn't tell him, she decided. The terror that she had felt that night was just too great. Camm and Cori both had tried to get her to speak with them. She had walked away from them as well, the two unsure as to where they stood with anyone.

Late that night, Dougal rubbed at his face, something that he seemed to be doing a lot lately. He was exhausted, fatigued, not sure how to describe how he felt. He roamed his house, checking locks and then heading for his rest. The other three members of his household had already retired. The man standing just outside the living room windows watched as the lights were extinguished before he stared at the envelope in his hand and then reached to tape it to the window, somewhere he was certain they would find first thing in the morning, before he walked away.

McKala had stood and watched Dougal, a frown on her face before she smoothed it away. She had no idea what that man had wanted. She had no documents, no financial information such as he had demanded. Retiring, she had listened to Dougal as he moved through the house and sighed to herself. She couldn't speak. Terror had done that. Whoever that man was, his threats of violence against her family and Dougal's family and friends if she spoke had removed that ability from her. God, where are You? Her heart cried out for His presence, for Him to work it out and remove the man and his threats. Verses of comfort, of hope, of protection, of safety, of peace flooded her mind but they didn't work.

Dougal reached to cradle his bride to him as his eyes closed and he slept. His sleep was restless as was McKala's. Dreams haunted both of them, driving McKala to rise in the early morning hours, to pace the house before she headed for the back deck and solitude. The others would be up shortly, the two young ones to be off for their activities on a Saturday. They had been taken in by the youth groups at the church, much to their delight. They were off somewhere that day on a trip, just where McKala couldn't quite remember.

Camm and Cori's excitement was very much in evidence an hour later as McKala watched them rush through their breakfasts, tidy up from their meal, hug her and then head off for the day. Deveney had watched them, smiles on her face before she approached McKala.

"McKala? Are you okay with them going away?" She was puzzled as were the others as to why McKala just refused to speak.

McKala had stared at her and then turned and walked away. Deveney sighed, knowing that she would be speaking with her brother. She turned as she headed for the door, stopping as she saw Holly and Lincoln heading up the walk.

"You two are here?" She was puzzled

"We are." Holly stared past her. "How are they?"

"Dougal was still sleeping, I think. I hadn't seen him. McKala is up, but still not talking." Deveney chewed at her lip before she shrugged. "I have no idea why."

"Terror, more than likely." Lincoln shared a look with Holly, reliving the adventure that they had shared, an adventure that saw Lincoln with amnesia, unwilling to harm the lady he had learned to love. "Let us speak with her. Maybe we can get through to her."

Deveney shrugged. "Go for it. And good luck with that. Somehow, I don't think it will work."

Lincoln watched as Holly walked up the stairs and into the house, looking for her long-time friend. He sighed. Holly had been very vocal the night before, worried about Dougal. She knew how she had felt when Lincoln could not remember who he was or why he was so afraid for her. Deveney hesitated and then shook her head, walking towards the waiting van. Lincoln hesitated to approach the house, searching the outdoors. Spying the envelope on the window, he sighed. No, he thought, today would not be a good day. He worried about Dougal. He knew that Holly was terrified for him, a man whom she considered to be the brother who she had never had.

Dougal stood on the porch, watching as Lincoln walked towards him. Extending the mug of coffee to the other man, he sipped at his own.

"What did you find?" Dougal's voice was low and rough. He was not having a good morning, he thought, and what Lincoln held in his hand wouldn't make it any better.

"This? It was taped to your front window." Lincoln studied it. "Who's looking after you today? James is away with the youth."

"No one." Dougal reached for it. "I have to open it, I guess. I just don't know that McKala will stay around for me to go over it with her."

"She's still not talking?" Lincoln drew a deep breath when Dougal shook his head, taking in the devastation on his friend's face.

———

Chapter 27

McKala stared at the paper that Dougal had shoved at her, not wanting to read it, but knowing that she had to. She glanced at it, finding the threatening words vicious but not as vicious or terrifying as the words that the man had spoken directly to her. She placed it back on the table and turned and walked away, leaving Dougal staring after her. He couldn't believe that she had just done that. Lincoln and Holly shared a look before Holly moved to follow McKala, stopping at the hand that Dougal laid on her arm.

"Let her go. She's not talking with any of us. None of us can even get a reaction from her." Dougal sought for a chair to sink into, his legs suddenly feeling very weak.

"She's terrified, Dougal. Something happened or was said to her when she was captive." Holly began to pace the floor, Lincoln watching her closely before he moved to follow McKala.

Lincoln stood and watched as McKala moved to a bench near the back of the yard. He had spoken with Dougal's friends who had given him advice and suggestions. Even at that, none of the men or their ladies had words of wisdom to really help Dougal. And that was something that Lincoln wanted to do, to help his friend. He didn't want to see him face what Lincoln or his brother and sister had done.

———

McKala shook for a moment, the fear driving her to that. She desperately prayed, asking for peace and wisdom. *Lord, You have promised that. You promised never to leave me, to hide me in the hollow of Your hand, to cover me as a hen covers her young. I need that. Dougal needs that. I have brought such danger to him and I don't know how to take it away. I am so afraid for him and for his family. If I didn't have to worry about Camm and Cori, I would never have agreed to marry him. I thought that would bring us safety. Instead, it has just brought danger to him.* McKala blinked rapidly, the tears clouding her vision, before she stiffened and stared behind her.

Lincoln moved rapidly towards her, a hand out to grasp her arm and pull her to her feet and back towards the house.

"Inside, McKala. Someone is out here. We need to get you inside." Lincoln shoved the door closed behind them, ducking his head to stare at the backyard.

"Lincoln?" Dougal was on his feet and beside his friend.

Lincoln shook his head.

"Someone was out there. McKala wasn't paying attention to her surroundings. She could very easily have disappeared again."

Dougal's gaze shifted to McKala, finding her watching him. He sighed. They needed to talk, but he didn't think that would be happening any time soon.

"The letter, Dougal?" Holly spoke from the kitchen doorway. "Did you call anyone?"

Dougal shook his head, his eyes not leaving McKala's face.

"No. I sent James a text. He'll stop in tonight when they're back." He grinned suddenly. "Apparently, he and Deveney are dating. They were keeping it low key."

Holly snorted, causing the two men to laugh.

"Not low key at all, Dougal. Everyone but you seems to know."

Dougal shook his head again.

"Just like with you two. They'll be working to solve this for us." He searched McKala's face, seeing the blankness on it. "McKala? We need to talk, darlin'. And talk we will."

Late that afternoon, Dougal wrapped Cori in a hug, grinning at how she was stumbling over her words. The excitement from the day's trip spilled over from both Cori and Camm. He nodded at James as he headed for the freezer and meat.

"Thanks, James. I think that we need to send these two to bed without any supper. They've had enough excitement for the day." He grinned wider at the protests from the two before they ran off, intent on finding their cousin and Holly.

James hesitated for a moment.

"Dougal? That letter?"

"Yeah, that letter." Dougal sighed. "McKala read it and then just walked away. She has to have been threatened somehow."

"I think that she was." James headed out of the door, his thoughts troubled. Ted had told him that he needed to talk with Dougal about a new finding in the case. Only he had no idea just how to do that. His prayer was that he would have the words he needed, but even with that prayer, he wasn't sure that he even would.

Two hours later, Dougal stood behind McKala, his hands on her shoulders. That was the only thing keeping her in front of him. James watched with compassion as she stared at him, not an emotion breaking through.

"McKala? You've read the letter. Talk to us. You need to tell us what happened when you were gone. You haven't done that." To say James was frustrated was an understatement. "I'm the investigating officer. I need to hear from you."

McKala simply stared at him, making not a move to speak.

Holly's hand on James' wrist brought his attention to his friend. Holly's eyes were on McKala, understanding in them.

"Who did he threaten, McKala? But it's more than that." Holly drew in a deep breath, her face blanching as she did so. "Who did he kill, McKala? Who did he kill in front of you? And then threaten you with the same."

Shocked, the two men exchanged a glance even as McKala broke free from Dougal and ran, the back door slamming after her. Holly was on the move, heading after her, leaving James to steady Dougal as his friend shook with shock. Camm and Cori stood beside them, horror on their faces.

"Dougal? Is that what happened? Is that why McKala isn't talking?" Camm and Cori clung to one another in their shock and fear.

Chapter 28

Holly approached McKala and then just sat beside her friend, her foot shoving the swing into motion. She had no words to say. Instead, she could only pray. *Is this what happened, Lord? He killed someone in front of her?* Holly frowned. She hadn't heard of any bodies being found in town, well other than McKala. Ted, the doctor's son and a good friend of hers even though he was just in his late teens, would have told her. She sighed. *How do we do this, Lord? How do we find out what happened and then work to keep these two safe? I need to talk to the other ladies, I think, and have them help.*

"Is that what happened, McKala?" Holly's voice barely broke through the early evening noise. She could hear the rustling of the critters, the cooing of the doves nearby, the twitter and chirps of the birds, the frogs in a nearby pond. She loved the area that Dougal had found for his house, on the outskirts of town, just still within the city limits.

McKala's motions of rubbing at her arms stilled as Holly spoke. She blinked rapidly, the tears that she had tamped down within her threatening to overwhelm her. Her emotions were all over the place. Part she knew was because Dougal had collapsed and she had not known for hours what had happened to him or even if he was still alive.

"McKala?" Holly's voice was soft. "Lincoln couldn't remember for a year who he really was or why he had come to Cairn. He had been asked to kill me, refused, and was beaten so badly he almost didn't survive." Holly's eyes were on McKala's face that had turned to her. "I was kidnapped. He was beaten again at the year mark and almost died on me. His brother and sister went through stuff as well. Larkin's husband almost didn't survive. He had been imprisoned for months. We have other friends who had have adventures as we term them. There's also Flannery, Ayron, and Breckon that you can talk to. Don't shut us out. God has brought you into our circle. We are praying for you. By keeping silent, you are doing what this monster wants you to."

McKala's brow furrowed for a moment before she sighed, the first audible sound that she made in days, she thought. Thank you, Lord, for Holly. She is honest and open. Dougal says she speaks the truth, unvarnished at times, but she is used by You in so many ways.

"Thank you, Holly." McKala's voice was hoarse from disuse. "You are correct. I am doing what he wants. He told me not to talk. That if I did, people I love or know would die. I am letting him win."

"Do you know who it was?" Holly reached for the pad of paper and pen that for some reason she had stashed in her jeans pocket.

"No, I don't. I never have. That's frustrating. He's chased me for so long, it seems." McKala blinked rapidly, feeling Dougal's arms come around her and shift her over even as Lincoln and James dropped to the ground in front of them. Camm and Cori ran to catch up with the men, knowing that something had just happened.

"McKala?" Dougal's voice was low, his breath wafting across her cheek.

"Dougal? I'm so sorry." Tears clouded her eyes even as his head bowed and he prayed, following in prayer by Lincoln and James. Deveney had appeared as James prayed, dropping down beside the two youngsters, arms around them.

James studied McKala, knowing that he needed to speak with her but he wasn't sure if she would answer any of his questions.

"McKala? I need to get your statement."

McKala nodded, not wanting to speak but knowing that she had to tell them what that monster had threatened and what he did.

"James? Did you find a body? A teenager?" McKala's voice was low and broken.

James' hand stilled for a moment as he stared at her before he shook his head.

"No, we didn't. And I haven't heard that any other detachment did. Why?"

"Because he killed a teenager in front of me. At least, I think he did." McKala's gaze raised to the sky and she followed the flight of some geese. "What if he didn't? How do I prove that?"

"Tell me what happened. Talk to me, McKala." James looked at Dougal, seeing the discomfort on his face and the fear in his eyes for his bride.

———

McKala twisted to look up at Dougal, seeing the fear for her in his eyes but also something else. Something that said that she was his and his alone. That she was beautiful and that he loved her.

Chapter 29

McKala prayed for strength to get through what she needed to. She searched the faces around her, seeing compassion, caring, and yes, worry. *Lord, I can't do this, but I must. This is when I need You to speak for me. I am so afraid for these ones here. Holly and Lincoln? I fear for their little one. That monster was so brutal in his words. I know that he will not hesitate to harm anyone who tries to help me. But I just don't get what it is that he wants. But You do. You have me in the hollow of Your Hand, covering me with Your other hand. Please, Lord?*

Her gaze dropped to James, finding him waiting patiently for her to speak. He nodded at the question on her face.

"Just talk to me, McKala." He held up his phone. "I will record it, take my notes, and then have it printed and you sign it. We can do that today. And yes, we all stay. I know it's not usually how it is done but we need to all hear what you have to say. Until I have you sign your statement, though. Once you have given it, you can talk about it. Do you understand?" He watched her closely, seeing her nod of comprehension.

"Okay, then. Let me just take a moment." McKala blinked rapidly, knowing that when she spoke, what had happened would be out in the open. That meant she could not protect the ones she loved and her new friends. She thought through what had gone on in the past, knowing that it all connected somehow. "I think it goes back to the accident, somehow, James. Only I'm not sure how."

"We'll look into that. I have asked for the accident report, McKala, Camm, and Cori. Only I'm told that there is none. That can't be correct."

"No, there is a report. I have a copy. At least I think I still do." McKala frowned. "Who hid it?"

"That's what we're looking into, McKala. Now? What happened that day?" James waited, then opened his mouth to speak again, catching the look on Dougal's face. His mouth snapped shut. *What is going on, Lord?* Dougal knows something or suspects something, doesn't he?

McKala drew in a deep breath, knowing that when she spoke, things would change. Her eyes rested on Camm and Cori. *Lord, protect these two young people. He threatened them in ways no one should ever have to try to protect them from. Lord? I can't do it. Not on my own. I've tried and it just hasn't worked out.*

"Okay, so, to go back to that day." McKala blinked back tears, knowing that if they fell, she would not be able to continue. "Dougal had collapsed. I was terrified. I thought he was dead."

McKala had dropped beside him, a hand on his back, rolling him over. Her head had gone down on his chest. A breath of relief wafted from her as she heard his heart beating but he was struggling to breathe. That much she knew. She was on her feet, racing for her phone, dialling for help. No, she stated, she didn't know what happened. He just went down and wasn't answering her. The anguish in her voice reached through to the dispatcher, who had looked around, seeking help.

Hearing a sound at the door, McKala was up, her feet carrying rapidly that way. She yanked open the door, expecting to see paramedics at the very least. She stared in horror at the man standing there, her hands reaching to slam the door shut. Only, that hadn't worked out. Not how she had wanted it to. His hands had reached for her, grasping her arms in a tight hold, and dragging her, kicking and screaming from the house and to a waiting vehicle.

McKala had fought to get away, just not able to do so. Handcuffs clicked on her wrists and a gag was pulled roughly across her face. Her eyes, huge with her fear, stared behind her as the house rapidly disappeared. The vehicle pulled over for the emergency vehicles racing towards them and towards Dougal. Only, she didn't know if he was still alive. Her fear was that he wasn't.

She continued to struggle, reaching for the door even though the car was moving at a high rate of speed. The man's hands on her distressed her. He was evil, that she knew. McKala was desperate to escape. When the vehicle finally stopped and she heard the locks click, she shoved at the door, fleeing from the vehicle and running towards the forest ahead of her, pulling the gag from her face. She heard the pounding footsteps behind her and then screamed as the man's body hit her and took her to the ground. Her breath was gone and she could not struggle, not for a moment. Yanked to her feet, her arm in a crushing grip, McKala was hauled back to the house and shoved inside, to a windowless room in the centre of the building. The cuffs were removed, the roughness of that very deed scraping at her wrists. The door was slammed and she heard the lock grating closed.

McKala had run to the door, yanking at the knob, banging on it, yelling for them to come back and let her out. Dougal needed her. She was in tears, begging them. She sank to the floor, huddled against the door, sorrow and despair in her heart. God, where are you? She cried out to Him, not feeling that He was there.

Chapter 30

Unable to sleep, McKala paced the room or slumped into a corner. The bright lights made the room hot and uncomfortable. She sighed. What did this man want? She had nothing that he would want. She knew that for sure. Anything of her parents or her aunt and uncle that were not sentimental to the three of them they had agreed to get rid of. McKala had done that. She despaired of evading this very man on their flight. Now, it didn't seem to have made much difference. She was in his hands and not likely to survive.

McKala was pulled from the locked room late one afternoon and dragged on reluctant feet to the office or whatever it was that he called it. She refused to look up at him, even when her hair was grasped roughly and her head yanked backwards. She heard the sounds of stumbling footsteps and peeked, seeing a youth standing in front of her, facing the man. McKala frowned for a moment, thinking that she knew the youth before attention was caught by the cruelty on the man's face.

Not comprehending what was being asked of her, McKala just shook her head. She jumped in fear as the weapon was pointed at her before her eyes closed. Dear Lord, this is it, isn't it? Today is the day that I graduate to heaven. Please, dear Lord? Don't let Dougal or Camm or Cori grief too much. Comfort them.

———

McKala jumped as she heard the sound of a muffled gunshot and screamed as she saw the widening red patch on the youth's chest. He stared in horror at her and then collapsed. The man turned to her, finding her horrified, terrified eyes on him.

"This is your fault, McKala. You just had to do what I asked. His blood is on your hands." He studied his nails before he turned and walked away.

Dragged from her chair, McKala was roughly shoved outdoors and towards a vehicle. Absolute terror shook her. She was next to die, she knew. Only where would that happen and when? Soon, she thought.

McKala was pushed roughly to the floor of the vehicle, a foot on her back holding her down. She prayed as she had never prayed in her life, fear lending wings to those very prayers. She felt no peace, no confidence that she would survive. Heal my family, Lord, McKala prayed. Don't let them grieve too long. She felt the prick of a needle on her arm and fought against it, her movements slowing and then stilling as she lose consciousness.

The man watched dispassionately as her body sagged and then lay still. He didn't care, not really. Only she had not told him what he needed to know. He would find it out, her family coming under his scrutiny now. She was useless.

McKala's body was dragged from the car and then carried to the chain link fence near the high school football field and dropped ruthlessly and carelessly. The man walked away without a backwards glance. He really didn't care if she lived or died. Dying was preferable, he thought.

McKala looked up at that point, tears clouding her eyes. She felt Dougal's arms tighten on her, her face burrowing against him as the relived horror flowed through her.

"What did he want, McKala?" James' quiet question broke the silence that had fallen as she had finished her words. He waited patiently, knowing that she needed time to compose herself.

McKala turned to him, a puzzled look on her face before she searched the faces of Camm and Cori. It pained her deeply that these two youngsters were suffering. She had no idea why.

"I don't know, James. I really don't. And if I don't, how do we stop him?" Her eyes slid closed as the tears that she could not control trickled down her face. She felt arms around her and hugged Camm and Cori, knowing that they were in danger. All her family had been threatened but the threats were so vague that she didn't know how to protect them.

Chapter 31

Dougal wandered his home once more late that evening. He needed to be seeking his rest but his thoughts were in too much of a turmoil. He wanted to avenge his lady, to find the man responsible and make him pay for what he was putting them through. Only, he had no idea who it was. McKala couldn't or wouldn't describe him, other than for vague hints and words. Dougal sighed, stress driving the fatigue that bogged his body down. He stood for a moment at Camm's doorway and then Cori's, watching them sleep, wishing and praying for relief for them from what they still faced.

Walking quietly to his own bedroom, Dougal hesitated, seeing the low lights on and knowing that McKala had already retired. Or at least, he thought she had. He moved to find his own rest, rolling over to tug McKala closer to him and just cradling her to his side. He felt her relax in her sleep as she felt safe, but he knew it was far from over. His eyes closed and he too slept, not realizing that the next few days would test their love for one another that was growing and also test their faith and trust in God.

McKala rose early the next morning, turning to study Dougal, seeing the whiteness of his face, the dark shadows, and sighed. *This is not working out so well,* she thought. *He wants to protect me and Camm and Cori, but he's just not well enough to. We need to talk, the two of us, but I am not sure I want to hear what he has to say. I just know that he'll tell me that he wants his freedom, that we brought too much trouble to him.*

Watching as the two youngsters moved quietly around the house, McKala turned at long last, heading for the outdoors and the swing on the back deck. She curled up on it, her eyes on her mug of tea. She didn't know why she had been targeted. James couldn't tell her either, even if he had a suspicion. She suspected that he did.

His phone in his hand, Dougal searched for McKala. It was Sunday morning, and he so desperately wanted to be in church, but he wasn't sure how she felt about that. He sighed. This was not easy. Not at all. He sent a swift text message to Deveney, telling her that they not likely would be there.

McKala looked up as a mug appeared in her line of sight and took it with a quiet word of thanks. She felt the swing shift as Dougal joined her, his foot sending the swing into slow motion. He just sat, content, he thought, to be with the lady who he loved so deeply. The quiet of the morning brought peace and comfort. They both needed that, he realized, his heart rising in prayer for his lady and her cousins and then for his own family.

"What's going on with James and Deveney?" McKala's words brought his head around to study her.

"James? Deveney? Why would you ask that?"

McKala stared at him and then shook her head.

"You don't know? They're dating, Dougal. And trying to keep it quiet. That could cause problems, you know."

"Dating? I didn't know that. How?" He waved his hand. "Never mind. I take your word for it. James would have talked to his supervisor, knowing him."

"He would have?" McKala drew a deep breath. This was not easy, she thought. She needed to remember what that monster wanted but she could not. "How did your friends do this?"

"My friends? As in Evan, Tag, and Shay?" At her nod, he paused, his thoughts drifting to what they had been through. "And Holly and Lincoln. And his brother and her cousin. And their sister and her now husband." He grinned for a moment. "Holly was adamant that Lincoln needed her. Did you know that her touch comforts him? That was what helped to get them through. And her father? You've met him?"

"Not yet, but she told me about him. How cruel for them to be separated like that!" Dougal bit back a grin at the anger in her voice. "I'm glad he's back. I so want to meet him."

"If we go to church, you can." His hand went up. "I know what you're going to say. That you will bring danger to everyone there. That's the thing, my love. Our town or village looks out for one another. They are watching out for you, Camm, and Cori. First, because that's what they do. Secondly, because you're my family." He reached for her hand, his head bowing for a moment. "I don't know that it will take to make you feel part of the family here, but that's what you three are. Now, if you don't feel up to church, we'll do our own."

"Camm and Cori have already taken off with Deveney. She was around before you were up. It's just us." McKala studied his profile, seeing his strength and determination to keep her safe. *Only, Lord, how does he do that? He's healing and I don't know that I can see him hurt again.*

"Then, we'll spend some time in prayer, my love, sharing our hearts and favourite Bible passages. Does that work?"

Chapter 32

The following Sunday, Dougal stood in front of McKala, a wide grin on his face, mirth sparkling in his eyes. She stood, hand on her hips, glaring at him, but grinning inside at the antics of the small gray tabby kitten sitting on his shoulder. Cori had found the little kitten and insisted on bringing her home for her own pet, only to have the kitten claim Dougal. The little one could be found wherever Dougal was.

"What?" Dougal continued to grin, even as he spoke.

McKala shook her head.

"Yes, we are heading to church this morning, Dougal. We need to. And no, the kitten is not coming. She will be fine at home."

"But she's just a baby!" Dougal reached for the kitten, scooping her into his hands before he wrapped McKala in a hug. "I know, my love. We'll leave her home. I just worry about you."

"Me?" McKala stepped back to stare up at him, wondering at how tall he was. She had always determined that she would not marry anyone that tall. *Lord, You let me. Are you telling me something here?* "But what about whoever it is that's after us? He's been around here, hasn't he?"

———

"I would suspect he has." Dougal bit at his lip in uncertainty. "Dad asked if we had considered getting a dog."

"A dog?" McKala walked away from him and then paced back. "A dog? Why?"

"For security, protection. It would alert us if someone was roaming around our home." Dougal studied her. "It was just a thought, McKala. We need to agree on this."

"I know." She bit at her lip, uncertainty on her face. She looked back up at him. "Do you have one in mind?"

"Not really. I have friends who have puppies but there is one friend who has an older puppy, not quite a year old, that he would like to re-home. He was keeping it for show purposes but it's gotten just a bit too big."

"Okay, we can discuss it. I know someone has been around." McKala wrapped her arms around her waist as she paced the kitchen. She spun, to find Dougal standing right behind her. "Dougal? How do we do this? Aren't we to be getting all kinds of threats, parcels, letters?"

He grinned for a moment. "You sound like the other ladies. We should be, but we're not. That tells me that someone is keeping a close eye on us. It will escalate, you know."

"That's what I am afraid of. How do we stay safe?" McKala watched Dougal closely, seeing the stress and worry he was trying to hide. "Dougal? When do you see the specialist again?"

"This week, Wednesday. You are coming with me." Dougal paused for a moment. "I don't understand something."

"And that would be?"

"I don't understand why you. What was he after?" Dougal searched her face.

"I'm not sure any more, Dougal. Not at all. I couldn't understand what he was saying, not really. He had a heavy accent." She looked up at him. "I had forgotten that. Did Camm or Cori mention it?"

"No, neither one did. But I don't think that they were close enough to hear him. Camm mentioned that you had told them to run and hide, that you would find them. He was scared that you would have disappeared that day and left them on their own."

"That still worries me, Dougal. What if something happens to me or to you? Who do they go to?" McKala paced the kitchen, not looking at him, not seeing the compassion on his face.

"Mom and Dad. Deveney. We can see the lawyer tomorrow and make it official. Dad had asked me just yesterday about that."

"They would do that?" McKala was not used to that kind of caring, not for years. Not until now.

"They would. They consider you all family and you are." Dougal glanced at the clock and then moved towards her. "We can ask them, but I know that they would say yes."

"Okay, so we ask. Now, how do we stay safe, Dougal?" She could feel the fear and yes, terror, rising in her.

———

132

"I don't know, my love. It's a day to day thing, isn't it? I'm off for now so when you're out and about, I will be with you. My fellow officers have offered to help as well. They are watching Camm and Cori for us."

"They are? I'm not used to that, you know." Dougal grinned at her disgruntled words. "But we need to start researching or whatever it is that you call it."

"And we will. Lincoln and Holly want to help. Lincoln has a friend who can help. She finds out so much about people. If we have some names, we can pass them on to her."

"She would do that? Without meeting us?" McKala was not used to friends like that. The few that she had had when younger were gone, moving on with their lives. That had saddened her and then made her reluctant to become friends with anyone. Dougal and Deveney were changing that for her, she thought. Their friends just moved in and enveloped her with their caring and compassion.

"She would, love. She would. Now, let's head out. I want to take my bride out for lunch, if she'll allow me that. It's a custom with our family that we do." Dougal watched her blink rapidly. "What did I say, McKala?"

"A family tradition. That's all. We hardly ever ate out, Mom, Dad and I. He was usually too busy with work to do that and he refused to eat out on Sundays, unless it was a special occasion."

Dougal simply swept her into a hug, feeling her return it.

———

"We'll start on our own traditions. If you're not comfortable with eating out, I'm okay with that."

Chapter 33

McKala turned as she heard her name called. She had escaped, she had decided, away from Dougal. He was starting to smother her, without meaning to. Needing a break from everything, she had headed for the downtown area on foot, needing that outlet of release.

Holly approached her on a run, reaching to give McKala a hug as she approached her.

"McKala! You're here and on your own. This must be my lucky day." Holly wrapped an arm around McKala and turned her to the store they were standing in front of. "And at my favourite store."

"It is?" McKala stared at Holly, not quite sure what was going on. "Aren't you working today?" She knew Holly worked as a landscape artist.

"Nope. I took the day off. I needed it. And I would like to spend it with you, or some of it, if I may."

McKala shrugged. "I guess. But I'm dangerous to know, Holly." She stared at her friend as she broke out into laughter.

"And so was I. Did Dougal tell you our story? What happened to Lincoln and me?"

Shaking her head, McKala sighed. "We haven't had that much time to talk. Not really. He's trying hard to protect me, even though he's not well enough."

"And he will. He was my best friend growing up. He was the brother I never had." Holly drew McKala into the store. "Let's shop, do lunch, and then we talk. You need a friend. God told me that today, sent me looking for you. And I found you."

"He does that?" McKala was not sure if that really happened in true life. She had never experienced it.

"He does. He sends people in to help others as they need it. It's up to them whether they accept His help or not. I pray that you are one who does."

"I would like that, Holly. I just wish this was all over." McKala's face shuttered for a moment. "I mean, any friends that I had before? I no longer have. They walked away from me when I took on Camm and Cori. And I couldn't say no, not for anything."

McKala was thoughtful as she walked back home later that afternoon. Dougal had sent a text message, just asking if she was okay and sending his love. She had stared at the message, not sure that was what he had meant. McKala looked around the town as she walked, liking what she saw. She knew that she would never go back to her home town. There was nothing there to take her there, other than the graves of her parents and her aunt and uncle. She could go and visit them, she thought, without living there.

A couple of hours later, McKala walked slowly home, her thoughts on the conversation that she had had with Holly. She didn't think that she had ever had such a conversation with a friend. It had been deep, thought provoking, and laden with God's promises of safety and protection. *Holly is so wise,* McKala thought. *She has been through so much. I don't know that I could have done what she did, marry someone who had amnesia. But then, that's Holly. She is such a wonderful lady who I am glad I can call a friend.* Lost in her thoughts, McKala didn't see the car trailing her.

Looking up, McKala's breath caught in her throat and she began to run. Yes, that was smoke rising from her home. But where was Dougal? The two youngsters had pleaded with her to let them stay with Deveney that night. They had called her when she had been eating her lunch. Holly had laughed at her, stating that Deveney was a wonderful lady who cared deeply for all of them.

A patrol officer stopped her forward rush with an arm around her before he turned her and pointed. His eyes scanned the area, searching for what it was he felt.

"Dougal's okay. He's over there." His finger pointed towards Dougal.

McKala broke free and ran towards Dougal, tears streaking down her cheeks. He turned slightly as he heard her running footsteps and caught her close to himself.

"Dougal?" McKala's voice was shaking from fear even as she clung to Dougal.

"I'm okay, love. I'm okay." His chin rested on the top of her head. "I got out without being hurt. The kitten's safe." He could feel the kitten moving around inside his shirt, finally poking her head out to look around.

"I was so afraid when I saw the smoke." She leaned back to look up at him, taking in the smoke streaking his face, the tears that had tracked from his red, swollen eyes. "You've been looked at?"

"I have, my love. I was just so glad that you weren't home." He looked around. "Someone is out here."

"I know. I felt someone following me all day. Holly looked after me."

"She did, did she? She's very creative in how she looks after people. She is known for that in town. She takes in strays and finds homes for them."

"She told me." McKala leaned against Dougal, a finger up to stroke at the kitten's head. "Now what, Dougal? Who did this?"

"James is working on that, he said. The investigation is just starting." He looked up as Duncan approached. "Dad?"

"You're okay, son? And McKala?"

"We are. McKala wasn't home." Dougal frowned. "But I don't understand how the fire started. We cleaned the chimneys just this past week."

"I know. Is that where it started?"

"That's what they are thinking. I had started a fire, just felt like it with the chilliness in the house. I went outside just to bring in some more wood and the house was full of smoke when I came back in. I don't get it."

"Someone has been around then, son. You told James and the patrol officer?"

"I did." Dougal sighed. "Now we have to find somewhere to stay for now."

"There's the guest cottage. Use it. The youngsters are welcome to stay with your Mom and I or with Deveney."

Dougal simply nodded, knowing that he and McKala would need to talk, but right now? All he could think of was holding onto her and trying to comfort her. He didn't see her studying him, taking in the dark circles under his eyes, the smoke and tear tracks on his face. He swayed slightly, fatigue hitting him.

"We need to get you somewhere, Dougal. You're almost out on your feet." McKala turned to try and find someone to help, freezing as she saw the man standing beside them, a weapon held on them in such a way that it was not visible to anyone else. "Dougal?"

"What, love?" When McKala didn't respond, Dougal's eyes dropped to her and then to the man standing in front of them.

The man motioned them away, watching intently to ensure that no one saw them. They were herded quickly to a car and shoved inside, the man sliding in beside them, his weapon on them.

Duncan stood where he had left the couple, staring around, a frown on his face. No, they weren't

there any longer. He spun in a circle, fear suddenly in
his heart.

Chapter 34

James stared at Duncan, not quite believing that Dougal and McKala had just disappeared.

"They can't be gone. They're here somewhere." James spun, searching for his friends.

"They're not, James. They've disappeared." Duncan moved away rapidly searching through the small crowd, not seeing his son and his daughter-in-law. Where are they, Lord? Duncan's heart was raised in questions. Where did they go and so quickly?

A hand on Duncan's arm stopped his search. He turned, finding Tag there.

"Tag? You're here?"

"I am. So are Evan and Shay. Where's Dougal?"

"He's disappeared. He and McKala. They were here. I had just spoken with them and then left to put their kitten in my car. When I got back not even five minutes later, they had disappeared."

"That's what I was afraid you would say. Word on the street as reached us, that this was a set-up to get to them." Tag's hand drew him away from the area, a nod directed at James.

"There was? How?"

"Brownie heard and couldn't reach Dougal. He reached out to Evan. We were all together, working on this when he called. The ladies are at Evan's, praying for them." Tag almost shoved Duncan into his vehicle, reaching for the keys. He watched as Duncan gathered the little kitten in his arms.

"Where do we search, Tag? This is hard, you know, when it's one of your own."

"We know, Duncan. That we know. Let's head for your place. James will bring them there if they come back here."

"But you don't expect them to." Duncan sighed. "This is not how today was to go, you know. I think they had an idea something like this would happen. They signed paperwork the other day making us all guardians if something happened to one of them."

"They did? That doesn't surprise me. Dougal's that careful."

"He is." Duncan sighed, his eyelids sliding down to cover the tears that he refused to shed. "How do I tell his mother and his sister? And how do we tell the youngsters?"

Abigayle stared at Duncan, hands covering her mouth, horror on her face.

"That can't be, Duncan. I talked to McKala a couple of hours ago. She said she was with Holly."

"She was." Duncan wrapped into his arms, watching as the three younger men headed for the kitchen. He could hear the water running and then the aroma of fresh brewing coffee. "I talked to them at the fire and then headed for my car with the kitten. By the time that I got back to where they were, they were gone. I don't know if anyone saw anything. James knows and is working on it."

Abigayle drew in a shuddering breath. "They've taken them. But who are they? Do we know anything?" She looked towards the door as the door bell rang. "Were we expecting anyone?"

Shay touched her shoulder on the way by.

"Emma and Abe were heading this way, I think. She had information that she wanted to give Dougal. I sent her a text to head this way instead."

Emma and Abe Finlay stood just inside the door, watching the older couple, seeing on their faces the worry and devastation that they had seen too many times before. But they also saw the peace on their faces that God was in control and had the young couple in His hands.

Abe looked up and around the kitchen after they had spent time in prayer, petitioning for Dougal and McKala. His hands cradled his coffee mug. He and his partner, Murphy, had a security team that had in the past worked security, even to the point of going in and retrieving people to bring to safety. Their focus had changed and they now did the training, although they would still go in and rescue ones who needed it. Evan and Flannery had felt their expertise at one point.

"Emma has information that she needs to share with you." Abe's voice was quiet and controlled, not letting his emotions show. "She has passed the same information on to James."

———

143

"I'm sorry, I'm not sure what you mean." Abigayle was confused.

"Let's just say, I look for people and find them and information that will help arrest them." Emma's smile was gentle as she reached for Abigayle's hand. "It's what I do, and no, I can't explain how I find people. I just do."

Duncan rose an hour or so later, stretching, before he walked through the house and out of the front door. He needed space, he decided, space to absorb what Emma and Abe had told them. It was not what he had expected. Not at all. He knew Deveney and the youngsters had headed for her home. He needed to check in on them but for now, he let it rest. Duncan watched as James walked away, fatigue weighing down each footstep.

"James?" Duncan reached to stop him, watching him closely. "You're beat and in need of food."

"I am and I do need to eat." James sighed even as he squinted at Duncan. There had been too many investigations in the last few days. This with Dougal? It had made it even harder. They were no further ahead.

"What can you tell me or can you?"

James shook his head.

"I need to speak with Dougal and McKala and can't. Until I can, our investigation has to stay as it is. You have had no word?"

Duncan shook his head, turning as he heard the door open behind him.

———

144

“No word. We’ve been working through stuff, stuff that Emma and Abe have brought to us. She said that you were given the same.”

“She did? Then it’s at the office waiting.” James sighed. “This wasn’t supposed to happen. They disappeared right out from under our noses. How?”

“I don’t know, James, but I know this. God is in control. We may seek vengeance for what they have gone through. But God is the Avenger. We need to leave it with Him, as hard as it is.”

“I know. I just wish it was different.”

Chapter 35

A week had passed since Dougal and McKala had disappeared. Searches had been made with no success. James had gone to his sources on the streets, again with little success. He wasn't sure if it was that people knew and wouldn't say or if they just didn't know. That concerned him.

Duncan and Abigayle were worried, particularly for Dougal. They had no idea if he needed the medication that kept him alive or not. They certainly didn't want to bury their son, not because of this. But they knew that he would do everything that he could to keep alive, to protect McKala. They were at a loss for words to comfort Camm and Cori. The two were devastated at losing McKala once more. Even being with Deveney didn't bring them comfort.

Looking up that afternoon, Duncan squinted at the man walking towards him. No, he thought, I don't know him. But he seems to be heading this way.

"Can I help you?" Duncan's voice brought the man's head up and he watched as he headed his way across the lawn.

"You can. You're Duncan?"

"I am. And you would be?"

The man's smile widened.

"Cautious. Evan said that you would be. My name is Doug Foster. I am a friend of Abe's, his cousin in fact. He asked me to head this way." Doug looked around, his keen eyes not missing much. "I am an officer, head of our local Emergency Task Force. Is there somewhere inside that we can talk?"

"There is. Come on in. I'm on my own for a change. Abigayle, my wife, and Deveney, my daughter, are at the church, meeting with the ladies. The two youngsters are in school." Duncan pointed to his office. "In there, I think, Doug. I have coffee if you wish."

"That would be great." Doug held up a parcel. "A friend's wife heard I was heading this way and sent some goodies as she calls them. She runs an Irish bakeshop and thought that her goodies might bring some comfort."

"Thank her for me. I am sure that they will." Duncan sank into his desk chair, feeling old and decrepit. His heart was hurting, and even though he knew God was in control, he still feared.

"May I pray first, Duncan?" Doug didn't wait for his consent, simply bowing his head to pray. When he finished, he hesitated before he raised his head. "Abe sent me with information for you. But he also asked that I tell you my story."

"You have a story? About your work?" Duncan watched him closely/

"I do. Darcy, my wife, and I were targeted by a rogue cop before we were married. He killed a number of people when he targeted various emergency services. In fact, he shot Darci and I almost lost her." Doug looked down for a moment, memories surging through him. "She survived. Darcy is a retired forensics psychologist and does profiling at times." He nodded to the package. "She has done that as well for Dougal and McKala. Copies of everything that is being provided to you have been sent on to James. In fact, I dropped it off earlier today.'

"I don't understand, though, why you are here." Duncan raised his mug of coffee, his hand shaking as he tried to sip at it.

Doug watched with compassion as the older man avoided his eyes.

"It's okay, Duncan. You're worried, stressed, not sleeping. I've been there, so I understand to a certain extent. A number of my friends have gone through stuff like this."

"Stuff like this? Quite the way to word it, Doug." Duncan sat back and watched the younger man, just older he thought than Dougal.

Doug laughed. "It is, but you know what I mean. Now, about Dougal? Any word at all?"

Duncan shook his head. "None whatsoever. And that is worrying. At this point, we still don't know if they are alive or dead. James has gone to the street, he says, but hasn't said what he heard."

"No, and he won't. Not unless he has to." Doug sat back, his eyes on the folder. "I am not privy to what Emma and Jace have found. That is for your eyes. But I know Emma is quite concerned."

———

148

"What would you do, Doug? As an officer such as you are, you must have some thoughts. Even on a personal level."

Doug thought for a moment and then began to speak. Duncan reached for a pad of paper and a pen, his hand flying across the notepad as he jotted down Doug's words. He sat back at long last, studying his notes and then the younger man.

"Would this work?"

Doug shrugged. "It's hard to say, but I know that you want to start somewhere. Start here. Talk to Dougal's friends. They'll be on board, I know. Listen, I have to run. If you have any more questions or concerns, call me or call Darcy. Our contact information is in the folder for you. In fact, I can almost guarantee that Darci will call you, your wife, and your daughter. She will want to speak with Camm and Cori as well."

Duncan nodded, then paled. "How much do we owe you, Doug? You can't be doing this for free."

"But you see, Duncan, we are. We consider you friends. Besides, you're part of the law enforcement community through Dougal. We take care of our own. This is how we do it." Doug was gone before Duncan could say another word.

Chapter 36

Lifting his head from the file that he was working on, James frowned and then was on his feet, heading out of his office door. He walked rapidly towards the patrol officer heading his way.

"Patrick? What do you have?"

"This!" Patrick held up an envelope. "I was handed it and told to give it to only you. I didn't recognize the youth. I don't think he's from town."

"Okay. Work with Susie on a sketch and then come find me. I want to hear your report." James studied the envelope before he headed for the crime lab. He didn't want to destroy any evidence if he could help it.

Back in his office a short while later, James sat in his chair, a frown on his face. Now, how does this find those two? He laid the letter down, the frown deepening. It didn't make sense, did it?

We have your friends. They won't be back. She has refused to cooperate. That has sealed their fate.

James drew in a deep breath. This is not what he had wanted to read. The lab tech had simply shaken his head. Ordinary paper and envelope were what he had stated. It was printed but that didn't even help if they didn't have the computer and printer that were used. James knew that wouldn't likely happen.

His brow furrowed as he thought through what he had discovered himself as well as what others had handed him. He sighed. He really wasn't any further ahead, other than for the feeling that time was running out for his friends and that they weren't in town. His hand paused as he reached for his computer keyboard and then he was on his feet, heading for the door, not seeing Ted walking towards him.

James groaned as his phone rang just as he opened his car door. He pulled it out, barking out his name.

"James? It's Dooley. Evan asked me to call you." Dooley's voice sounded hurried, and James could hear the sound of pavement over the phone.

"He did? Why, Dooley?" Dooley slid into his car and pulled out of the lot.

"He thinks that he knows where Dougal and McKala are. Somewhere between Dougal's town and here. In McKala's home town."

"Her home town? We spoke with a detective there. He didn't seem to think that she would be. She had sold her house. Or did she?" James' voice died away. "Dooley? Do you know if she had? I was under the impression that she hadn't. Not yet."

"That's what we thought. We looked into the detective. He's been sidelined by a shooting. He's being investigated. That makes us think that her house has not been sold." Dooley paused. "I talked to the chief there. He was very disturbed, to put it mildly. He knew her parents and her aunt and uncle. His comment was that she wouldn't have sold the house, not like it has been noised around. He was going to look into it and get back to me and to you."

"Okay. So, are they there?" James sighed to himself. This was just getting bigger and bigger, wasn't it, Lord? Please, Dear Lord, keep my friends safe.

"That's what we wonder. I'm off tomorrow and heading that way."

"Okay. I can clear my day to do the same. I will meet you there." James pulled to a stop in front of Dougal's house, staring at it. *Where are you, my friend? Are you even still alive? We need to find them, Lord, only I have no idea where to search.*

Chapter 37

Staring at the house or what remained of it the next morning, James' heart sank. I just pray, dear Lord, that they were not in it. The house was in ruins, smoke still sifting towards the sky. It had to have burnt yesterday, James thought. He studied the yellow police tape surrounding the area and sighed. This had just complicated his investigation, he thought. Lord, where are they? Are they here and no longer alive? Or are they hidden somewhere else? He looked around as he heard a vehicle and then moved from his to approach it.

"Dooley? This is not looking good."

Dooley stared at the house and then at James.

"No, it's not. I spoke with the fire chief. He didn't think that there was anyone inside when it burnt, but they still have to search." He paused. "I did hear that they arrested a youth coming out of the house as the emergency personnel arrived."

"And has he said anything?"

"It's a she, and not that I am aware of." Dooley looked around. "I didn't know that McKala lived in the country."

"I don't know that we ever discussed it. And we should have. There has just been too much going on with Dougal." James headed around the edge of the yard. "It's an old place, but looks as if it was well maintained."

"It does, going by the garage. That must have been a drive shed at one time." Dooley paused. "You know, if it's an old place, there would have been a cistern. Abandoned by now."

The two men shared a look and then separated to start searching. The patrol officer assigned to duty there watched them and then approached James.

"Sir? May I see some identification?'

James spun at his words and then pulled out his wallet.

"This place belongs to the wife of a good friend. They are both missing" James searched the area with his eyes, watching Dooley as he walked the side of the yard.

"And you think that they are here?" The patrol officer handed back the wallet. "We don't think anyone was inside the house."

"No, I don't think there would be." He watched as Dooley stopped and then ran for his vehicle, returning with a large flashlight. "He's found something."

"A cistern, no doubt. The chief knows this property. I don't know that we knew McKala was missing or had married. What about Camm and Cori?"

"They're with Dougal's parents and safe. It's a story in itself how they married. Dougal almost died from a gunshot and then collapsed from a blood clot. He's not well enough to go back on patrol."

———

"He's an officer?" By this time the two men had arrived at Dooley's side.

"He is. A colleague of mine. Dooley, what did you find?"

"The cistern. The covering boards look as if they have been disturbed" Dooley turned to stare at the patrol officer. "Was this searched?"

"Not that I am aware of. The concentration last night was on the house and containing the fire. What do we have?"

"Let's get some of these boards out of the way." Dooley was on his knees, reaching for his light to shine it around the cistern. It stopped abruptly. "They're here. Down there. We need a ladder."

The patrol officer, Thomas by name, ran for the garage. He remembered seeing a ladder in the garage, which to their surprise was unlocked. Grabbing it, he moved quickly back to the two other men. The ladder was lowered and James was down it, staring at McKala who lay sprawled facedown. His hand was shaking as he reached for her wrist, his head dropping in relief as he felt her pulse. James turned as he heard scuffling from behind him and watched as Dooley assessed Dougal.

"Dooley?" James was almost afraid to speak.

"He's alive, James, but in rough shape." Dooley studied the chains holding Dougal to the wall. "We need to get rid of these chains and I am not sure how."

Thomas looked down at them, watching intently as they spoke,

"I have teams on the way. Dooley? You said chains?"

Dooley looked up. "I did. There is a lock on them but I'm not sure if we can even release them to get him away from the wall. They have certainly wound them around him. Have they been here all the time?"

James spun on his heel, searching the area.

"That I wouldn't know." James laid his hand on McKala's back. "They may have been. They're in rough shape."

James and Dooley watched as the pair were assessed, raised from the cistern, and then their stretchers wheeled to the waiting paramedic rigs. James rubbed at his face.

"I need to call Duncan."

"You do. You head in with them. I'll stay here and see what I can determine." Dooley sighed, echoing the sentiment that he could see on James' face. "It's not easy, James, and not likely to get any better. We need those two to tell us what happened, and I am not sure when or even if they will be able to."

"That's my fear, Dooley. That they don't survive." James walked away on that, his shoulders slumping. He knew that Duncan and Abigayle would be there as soon as they could. Deveney was away that day, taking the youngsters with her. He needed to call her but it wasn't his place. That would have to be Duncan that did that.

Chapter 38

James stared glumly down at his meal as he slid into a chair in the hospital cafeteria. He needed to eat, he knew, but had no appetite for it. Constant prayers were raising for Dougal and McKala and for the investigator. Dooley was on his way in, a text message letting James know that. James had been around to speak with Duncan and Abigayle but they had had no word other than the young couple were in the care of physicians. That frustrated them all. Deveney had been in touch, stating simply that she and the youngsters were on their way in. What could she do for him, she asked. He had smiled at that. Deveney put others first, he thought, and he loved that about her.

The sound of a tray hitting the table across from him raised his head and he stared at Dooley before he blinked. His gaze moved to the man sitting beside Dooley and nodded. Austin was there and he knew him.

"Austin? You're the investigator?"

"I am, James. I was just handed it. I feel like I am so far behind." His head bowed for a moment before he looked up, a blessing asked over his food. "Let's eat, even though we don't feel much like it. Then, we'll talk." He shared a look with Dooley

"Any word, James?" Dooley's voice was quiet, almost too quiet as if he feared to hear that neither one of the young couple had made it.

"I talked to Duncan just before I came down here There was no word yet. I told him I'd be back." James sighed. "I hate this, you know. We went through this with Holly and Lincoln, although not as bad physically. It was his memory loss that drove the investigation."

"I've spoken with them. It certainly did." Dooley finally pushed aside his tray, his note pad out "Now, where do we go? Dougal can't help us, not right now."

"Do we have any information as to what happened?" Austin studied the two officers with him.

"Not a lot. They just seemed to disappear without any sign or word." James sipped at his coffee, grimacing at the taste. "We've been looking for them and not finding anything in our town. This would explain why. What do you know, Austin?"

"Not a lot. The techs are going over the cistern. The assumption is that they were there the whole time. Dougal would have been chained to the wall to keep him from escaping or helping McKala to escape." He sighed as his phone chimed and then he excused himself.

"I don't like this, Dooley. Something is missing. Someone knows something."

"I know." Dooley's eyes were on Austin. "What do you know about Austin?"

"Not a lot, I would say." James gathered his garbage and stood, heading for the exit.

Dooley was at his side, not seeing Austin watching them, a closed look on his face. If he had, perhaps future events would have played out differently.

Both men, of strong faith, knew that God was in control, that He had protected their friends and kept them alive. They just didn't understand why.

James stood next to Dougal, watching his friend, not seeing any movement from him. He was afraid suddenly, afraid that his friend wouldn't come back to them. He turned as he felt an arm around his shoulder. Duncan stood beside him, bringing comfort to James.

"Duncan? Any word?"

Duncan nodded. "He's dehydrated. No real abuse other than from his struggles to escape. I was told that you found him chained to the wall."

James hesitated before he spoke, his voice breaking slightly.

"We did, Duncan. It is only speculation as to why."

"And I think I know why. To keep them from escaping." Duncan studied his son, seeing the dark circles under his eyes, the sunken cheeks, the whiteness of his skin. "I was told that they were likely rained on at some point. No hypothermia, though. God had them in His hands." He looked behind him at the door. "They are concerned about the blood clots, but so far the physician said they don't see any new ones. That is an answer to prayer."

"That it is." James bit at his lip. "McKala?"

"She's about the same. She has been awake but not talking much. The investigator was speaking with her but she isn't speaking with him. She knows him, she told me, and won't talk to him. What's going on there?"

"I have no idea. I know of Austin, have met him in the past. McKala will need to explain herself." James walked away at that point, heading for McKala to speak with her. Only, that didn't happen. She was sound asleep and he didn't have the heart to awaken her.

Chapter 39

McKala roused late that night, her eyes opening as she sought for the men responsible for their capture. She breathed a sigh of relief as she saw that she was safe, she prayed. *Lord, did You do this? Did You send someone to find us? I know someone asked me about Austin. I can't talk to him. Anyone else, but not him. No one knows what I have seen him do. I just don't get it, how he made it on the force. He says that he is a Christian. I don't want to judge him, that's not my place. But You know his heart, Lord. Is he for real or not?*

She slipped from the bed, searching for her clothing. Clean clothes, she thought. Abigayle or Deveney had been around. Closing the room door behind her, McKala crept down the hallway, avoiding the nurses and searching for Dougal. Please, Lord? Let him be on this floor. I don't want to be wandering all over. She paused at a doorway and then glancing around entered it. Dougal? Oh, my love! What did they do to you?

Her feet led her to stand beside his bed, a hand coming out to rest against his cheek. She could feel him turn towards her.

Dougal roused slightly, his eyes barely opening as he fought to awaken. He lost that fight, slipping back into the well of darkness that had enveloped him. He didn't respond to McKala's quiet calls, the heartbreak that she was feeling evident in her voice.

McKala looked around and then simply crawled up beside him, wrapping her arms around him as best she could. Unable to stay awake, her eyes closed and she slept, not hearing the quiet footsteps of the nurse as she came in. The nurse paused, shook her head and then reached to rouse McKala, pausing as she heard footsteps behind her.

Duncan stood there, his eyes on his son and then on the nurse.

"I don't think it will hurt, nurse. They have been through too much to be separated. Can we just let them be for now?"

The nurse was angered and shook her head.

"No, that's not happening."

Duncan stepped into her way, preventing her from reaching McKala and removing her from the room. That earned him a hateful glare. His eyes raised to stare behind her, finding the physician and a police officer, high in rank, he thought, approaching them.

"What's going on here?" The physician's voice was stern as his eyes moved between Duncan and the nurse.

"She can't be in here. She needs to be in her own room. Those are hospital rules." The nurse just refused to back down.

Duncan stared at her and then his eyes went to McKala. A frown briefly flitted across his face.

She's awake, he thought, and trying to figure out how to do this.

"We keep them together. If necessary, I will remove them from here and take them home. In fact, I think that is the best move." Duncan's phone was out as he called Ted, putting in his request, a request that Ted had already anticipated. "I just spoke with the police chief in our town. He has a private ambulance here to take them home."

The physician nodded. "Let me have a few moments and then that's what we'll do. Your family?"

"They're on the way home. I waited as did a friend of ours, a retired paramedic." Duncan stared at the police officer. "I would say that this investigation here has been compromised. To not have fully searched last night is not acceptable."

The police lieutenant nodded in agreement. He had spoken with Austin and found that he had not sent the teams to search properly and refused to say why. Austin had been removed from the case and that was why the officer was there. He couldn't say that he blamed Duncan for taking the steps that he was.

McKala sighed with relief as she settled down in the ambulance, her eyes on Dougal. He had not roused at all with the move and that worried McKala. Duncan watched through the front window, knowing that Everett, their friend, was back there and watching out for the young couple. But Duncan knew that they were in good hands. Ted had hand picked the team, friends from church.

McKala turned her head the next day as she heard James' voice. She knew that he would want to hear their story. Only she didn't have much of one to give.

James sank gratefully into an upholstered armchair, his body and mind sore from what he had been dealing with. Somehow, he thought the murder that he had been called into the night before related to McKala and Dougal. Only he wasn't sure how, and that was unusual for their town. He could hear Holly and Lincoln and knew that their little one was around somewhere, likely where McKala's kitten was.

"James? You're here?" McKala, always quiet, was even quieter. *She was subdued,* James thought, *and that was not her.*

"I am, McKala. I need to find out what happened. Dooley and I are the ones that found you along with a patrol officer named Thomas."

"Not Austin? I won't speak with him. I know him. He was just ahead of me in school and skirted around the edge of things. I don't trust him."

"No, you don't have to speak with him. He's been taken off the case and from what I understand is off on leave."

"Just great!" James stared at McKala. "Now, he'll come an find me." McKala looked up, fear on her face, not seeing Dougal heading her way, his walk shaking at best.

"And that would be bad because?" James shared a look with Dougal and then Dooley who had helped Dougal to the couch.

"Because he's involved. Somehow or other, I think he's involved. It was his older brother that has been hounding me." McKala blinked rapidly at the tears. "God help me, it was his brother, Angus, who was behind my problems. I didn't know that until now." Her face turned into Dougal's shoulder as he simply wrapped her into his arms and held her as she wept.

The three men stared at one another, grim looks and stern lines on their faces. They had a name now, but where would it lead them? And it was guaranteed, Dougal thought, that there were more people behind this.

Chapter 40

Moving slowly through his house late that afternoon, Dougal was deep in thought. He could hear the youngsters bickering in the kitchen, something unusual for them. He paused as he approached the doorway to the sunroom. McKala stood at the doors to the back deck, a dejected slump to her shoulders. Dougal walked quietly over to her and just simply wrapped her in his arms, content to stand and hold his grieving bride. And grieving she was, that he knew. He was.

"McKala?" Dougal finally spoke, his head tilting to study her face.

"Where do we go from here, Dougal?" Her eyes were bright with unshed tears. "We don't know who all it is, not yet. And it is only getting worse. This was meant to kill us."

"I know it was, McKala, but I am not sure which one of us it was directed at." Dougal stared through the door at the blackened pile of burnt wood off to one side. His father had made arrangements for the deck to be rebuilt. "The fire? That was a warning, I think. I don't think we were meant to be taken that day. They blocked the chimney and then set fire to the deck."

"That's what I don't get." McKala turned slightly as she heard the doorbell and then Cam heading for the door. "Were we expecting anyone?"

———

Dougal shrugged before he turned her and headed that way. "Not that I know of." He paused, his eyes on the couple in front of him. "Abe and Emma?"

"Dougal." Abe reached to shake Dougal's hand and then moved aside so that Emma could hug him as best she could, seeing that he had not released McKala.

"McKala, this is Abe Finlay and his wife, Emma. He runs a security team. She finds people through her investigation firm."

"You do?" McKala watched Emma closely and then moved towards her, a hand tucked around Emma's arm. "You just might be able to help. I need someone to look up some people for me."

"And I can certainly do that." Emma grinned at Cori. "I met Camm, I think it was. You must be Cori."

"I am. McKala? It's almost supper time. What we were to have? And Abe and Emma have to stay, don't they?" Cori worried her bottom lip, a new habit that she had picked up.

Emma reached out an arm and drew Cori to her, a glance behind her at Abe.

"We're not fancy, Cori. Not at all. Soup? Sandwiches? Whatever you make works for us."

Abe shook his head at Emma's nonsense, knowing what she was up to.

"Emma's right, Dougal. We're not fancy. And you know that we had an adventure as we term it as

———

did my seven guys and a number of friends. Now, where can we sit and talk?"

Dougal pointed to the office. "In there, I guess. Come along, Camm. You've been designated as one of the guys. Maybe you'll have an insight into your town that we need." Dougal frowned, a thought passing through his mind. "Somehow I think it all goes back to there, but I'm not sure how I got involved."

"Just by being there and who you are. That's all it takes, Dougal. God placed you there." Abe dropped the folders that he had been holding onto the coffee table and turned in a circle. "I like this, Dougal. Your home is welcoming. But I understand that you had a fire."

"We did. Arson. Didn't do a lot of damage but it was used against us. That's when we disappeared." Dougal stared at Camm for a moment. "Camm? What are your thoughts?"

"My thoughts? I don't know what you're asking." Camm's brow wrinkled as he tried to understand what Dougal was asking.

"I think that Dougal would like to know how you're feeling, what you experienced, what you saw or thought you saw, what you heard. That kind of stuff." Abe grinned at Camm and watched as Camm thought through his words and then grinned in response.

"I see." Camm was up and running from the room, returning in short order with a notebook. "Here. This is what I've done. Dad would have told me to. He told me once when I was having bad dreams just to write them down. And then we went over them."

Dougal nodded, his eyes on Camm, not seeing the looks Abe was throwing his way.

"Good man, Camm. Now, we'll look through it. But first, we need to pray and pray hard. This is where it always gets difficult and dangerous." Abe was as good as his word, leading them right to the throne of God.

Dougal wiped at the tears which he could not control, an arm coming out to wrap around Camm.

"Thank you, Abe." Dougal looked towards the doorway and just beckoned Cori to him, wrapping her in a hug as well. "All set for dinner, Cori?"

"We are. And then can we pray too?" Cori's woebegone look tore at the men's hearts and they shared a look, both determined to find the culprits and end the adventure as it was termed soon.

Chapter 41

Later that evening, Dougal stood and stared down at the mass of material that Abe and Emma had left for them. She had simply stated for them to go over it and then call her. She was still working through what was going on, pulling names and addresses and sending them on to James and his team. Dougal shook his head. He had no idea how she was finding what she was but he was grateful. It was starting to make sense, sort of, he thought. His prayer was that it would be over soon and they could go on with their lives.

McKala watched him for a moment before she approached him, a hand touching his back. He simply reached to hug her to him, feeling the shudders of fear in her as she stared at the material.

"Will this solve it, Dougal?" McKala's voice held hope, hope that at long last she would be free of whoever it was that was after her and that she could finally understand why.

"I pray it does. Emma and Jace in her office will continue to dig. Abe said that one of his men's wives would be digging into the family tree. That's what she does." Dougal's chin rested in her head, his eyes staring towards the darkened sky that he could barely see. "We need this over, McKala. We need to go on with our lives and this is hampering it."

McKala drew in a deep breath. What was he meaning?

"Dougal?"

Dougal sighed, knowing that he had to own up to his feelings and not sure that she was ready to hear them.

"I love you, McKala. More than anyone. More than I thought I could ever do. God placed me where you needed me. He knew that we would marry and then fall in love. At least I hope we do. I hate to see you hurting."

McKala's breath stilled for a moment before she drew in a deep one. He loved her. It was not one-sided after all.

"I love you too, Dougal. I was just so afraid that you didn't love me. I was ready to move on."

"I know you were." Dougal studied her face and then bent his head to kiss her. "I do love you, sweetheart. Now, we just to solve this and we can go on with our lives."

"I won't let him have control like that, Dougal." McKala broke away from him and began to pace. "We live our lives, Dougal. Not in fear. We can't. It's not fair to any of us if we do." She pointed to the material that Emma had left with them. "We go through that. Your friends I know will help. So will your parents."

Dougal had been watching her and agreed.

"That we will but right now, sweetheart? It's late. The youngsters have retired already. Tomorrow is Sunday, and I would like to be in church, if you wish."

"I need that." McKala almost ran to throw herself into Dougal's arms. "We all do. Can we do that safely?"

"That we can do our best to accomplish." He was content just to hold her. "Dad will want to know what we have discovered. We also need to talk to James. There is something off about this whole thing."

"I know. It's like they, whoever they are, are after us but it just doesn't make sense. You, I could see from your work. But me or the youngsters? That I don't see. We weren't rich. We had not hidden fortune or whatever it is that they seem to think we had."

"I know why." They turned as they heard Cori. She was across the room and in her cousin's arms. "I know why. I just forgot. It's all my fault."

"Cori? What are you talking about?" McKala stared at her cousin and then up at Dougal.

Dougal maneuvered the ladies to a sitting position on the couch and then sat on the coffee table, his hands reaching for Cori's as he prayed for her.

"What do you mean, Cori?"

Cori was unable to speak for the sobs shaking her. She didn't see Camm approaching and then sitting beside her, uncertain of how to react. McKala's hand reached to rest on his shoulder.

"Cori?"

Cori finally looked up at Dougal and his heart broke at the look on her face.

"I found something six months ago." Her brow wrinkled as she thought back. "It was a box of some kind. I didn't open it. It was metal and decorated. I left it in the garage but I don't know if it's still there."

"Where did you find it?" McKala shared a look with Dougal. She opened her mouth to speak again and then clamped it shut. They needed to let Cori speak as she could.

"At the back of the yard. It was just so weird that it was there." Cori turned to face McKala. "It was at the path that we always took to the pond. No one should have been there."

Dougal's face tightened and he reached for his phone, sending off a text to Evan and Tag.

"Evan and Tag will head there and find it. Whereabouts did you put it?"

"There's a hidden door right beside the work bench. In there." Cori rested her head against McKala. "I'm sorry."

"It's not your fault, Cori. You wouldn't have known. That's about the time that we had to go on the run." McKala hugged Cori, her eyes on Dougal, a question in them.

Dougal nodded. "We'll pray hard, Cori. If they know that you found something, then you're at risk. We'll need to make plans."

"And we will. Tomorrow. Off to bed, Camm and Cori. God is in control, just remember that."

———

McKala watched as they walked away, her thoughts troubled.

Dougal wrapped her in his arms.

"This is where it will get very hard, sweetheart. How do we keep them safe?"

"I know." McKala bit at her lip. "You searched in here for whatever it is that they seem to leave?"

"We did." Dougal gave a quick grin. "Many times and by more than one person. My fellow officers want this over."

"Dougal? What happens if you can't go back to being a patrol officer? What will you do?"

Dougal shifted his weight on his feet, knowing that McKala had asked the very question that he had been trying to avoid.

"I don't know, sweetheart, but we'll figure it out."

Chapter 42

A month had gone by. Dougal realized that they were no closer to finding out who it was, other than for Angus. Austin had been in touch but McKala refused to speak with him. Austin had spoken with Dougal but Dougal had not been forthcoming with him. He knew that McKala didn't trust him, but he just didn't know why.

Cleared to return to duty, Dougal was hesitant to do that. He loved his patrol work but worried about McKala and yes, Camm and Cori as well. Would they be safe? His love for the three of them but particularly McKala had grown over the past weeks. McKala challenged him but in a good way, he thought, driving him deeper into the Bible to prove or disprove what she asked him. They had spirited discussions, with Camm and Cori joining in. At first, the two had been reluctant to, seeming to think it would be challenging his authority as the head of the family. Dougal had explained it to them in a way that they understood, that he didn't see it as a challenge as they thought of it but it was a challenge for him to learn more and dig deeper and then to share with them. He encouraged them to do the same.

Tag had retrieved the box that Cori had found. It had contained paperwork that he refused to show her, instead handing it over to James. She had been put out at that, thinking that she needed to know, but

James had explained to her that it was evidence in their case and he just couldn't share it with her.

James had been around that morning, just to talk with them. McKala had stood, arms wrapped around herself, as she had listened, no expression on her face.

"McKala? Do you understand what I am saying?" James was frustrated, to say the least. This case was going cold, but he knew his friends were still at risk. He and Ted had talked about it. With Dougal going back on duty, that made it even more concerning for them.

"I do. You tell me that my house was burned down deliberately, destroying whatever was in it. But you have no idea who or why." McKala blinked rapidly, not wanting to shed the tears that clouded her eyes. "I can tell you how. Angus. He has always been watching me. I feel unsafe around him. Only I don't know why. And he is here in our town. I can feel him when I am out and about."

"Then, how do we do this, McKala? How do we keep you safe? Keep Camm and Cori safe?" James turned and paced away, coming back to stand in front of her. "We need to dig deeper into this. Only I have no idea who to look for or even why or what."

McKala stared at him before she walked away, heading for the office.

James stared after her before his gaze turned to Dougal and he pointed after her.

"Did she really just do that?"

<hr>

176

"She did, James. She's terrified and trying not to show it." Dougal's hands went through his hair. "Holly told me that she would be. She's been talking with McKala as has Emma and those of Emma and Abe's friends that McKala will speak with. She's also talked to Lincoln's sister, Larkin."

McKala was back, a sheaf of papers in her hands.

"This is the latest that Emma and Kat have sent to me. Dougal and I have gone over it. She has given names that I don't know or recognize. Any that I have? I've marked and said why. It doesn't make sense, James."

James searched her face as he reached for the papers, seeing the fear in her eyes that she was trying to hide but also the determination to solve their mystery and soon.

"Don't put yourself out there, McKala."

McKala stared at him, not backing down.

"If that is what it takes, I will, James. Dougal and I have discussed it. We are going nowhere with this. We need it over." McKala blinked rapidly, opened her mouth to speak, and then spun, almost running from the room.

"Dougal?" James turned to Dougal, finding him staring after McKala, devastation on his face.

"James, she's right. We have discussed it. We are not closer to finding out why or who. And if that is what it takes, then we are agreed. Dad and Mom are on board with us. Deveney is not sure but she wants to protect Camm and Cori." Dougal drew in a deep breath. "It is our fear that they will use Camm and Cori against McKala."

"That they will. Is there any way to send them somewhere for a few weeks?" James was running scenarios in his head.

"Abe and Emma have offered to take them in, if it comes to it. Eunice and Everett as well. But that couple is too close to us. If we have to, Lincoln's brother or sister will do that. They actually live in the same town as Emma and Abe."

"I see. Make your plans, Dougal. We need to have something in place." James paused, a thought crossing his mind. "Abe has a security team, right?"

"He does and he has friends that would step in. He has also offered to contact a friend in another town to see if they would help."

"Sounds as if you have things moving ahead." James looked at the floor for a moment. "But you, Dougal? How do we keep you safe when you are out on patrol?"

"I talked to Ted. I'm moving into the detachment for now. Working a desk. I'm not happy about that but it is what it is."

"I see. That will help." James turned away to stare out the living room window and then was running from the house.

Dougal moved rapidly to the door, watching as James tackled a man who had been standing on their front lawn. McKala was beside him, her hand covering her mouth.

———

178

"What is Austin doing here? He shouldn't be. Dougal? Is he involved?"

"I would think so. I just got word that he has been suspended from the force and that he blames you. James will sort it out or at least I hope that he will."

Chapter 43

Dougal stared at James later that day. He had returned, wanting to specifically talk with McKala, who in turn stared at him as well.

"Just what are you saying, James?" Dougal was puzzled as to his friend's words.

"Austin is no longer an officer. The suspension is permanent. He has been charged with arson, McKala. He is the one who burned down your home. He thought he would draw you back to town. Only, someone else had brought you back. He can't or won't tell us who he is working for."

"So, we're not really any further ahead?" McKala paced, her face thoughtful. "I wonder."

"You wonder what, sweetheart?" Dougal deliberately stepped into her path, causing her to stop.

"Their father. He was around Dad's age. Dad never like him but never said why. He was in the bank, a financial advisor at one time. Is that why?"

James stared down at his notes, knowing that somehow this had been missed.

"I don't think that we ever looked at their family. And we should have." He looked up as McKala snorted. "McKala?"

"Check your email, please. Emma has found a wealth of information on him, pun intended. She just

———

180

let me know this morning." McKala walked away, frustrated at the turn of events.

"James?" Dougal's voice was quiet.

"Yeah, I know, Dougal. I wasn't the one working on that. Someone else was. I'll need to talk to Ted."

"Do more than talk. This is destroying her. She is not certain now if it was just an accident or something worse that took her parents and her uncle and aunt. Find out what it going on. And do it yesterday." Dougal's words had a bite to them, not usual for him.

James agreed with him and headed off, his thoughts muddled for a moment. He pulled to the side of the street, his phone out, searching for a name. There. That was who it was, wasn't it, Lord? Pulling back onto the road, he never saw the truck approaching him. His car spun from the impact and landed against a tree, James slumped over the wheel. The truck disappeared, damaged and all.

Onlookers ran for James's car, prying open the door and reaching for him. The emergency personnel simply shook their heads. How did this happen?

Dougal stared at Deveney as she stood in front of him, her face covered with tears, twisting at the engagement ring that James had placed on her finger just days earlier.

"It can't be, Deveney. He was just here." Dougal's hands rubbed at his face.

"It is, Dougal. He was hit not far from here. I need to go to the hospital. Will you come? Mom and

Dad are away." She looked past her brother at McKala, who stood with a horrified look on her face. "McKala? Will you come with me?"

"Absolutely. Dougal?" McKala was across the room, her arms around her sister-in-law, heading for the door.

Dougal simply swept the ladies outside and into his vehicle. This is not what he had expected. Who, Lord? Just who is it? We're getting names and relationships to one another, but no clear idea or evidence to say who. Or do we?

An hour later, Deveney walked back towards where her brother stood, tears on her face, sobs shaking her body. Dougal simply held her as he had when she had been young and needed comfort. McKala's hand rubbed at her back.

"Deveney? How is he?" McKala's quiet voice and question finally reached through the despair that Deveney was feeling.

"I don't know. Joe said that they were still assessing him. Imaging and whatnot is how he put it. But he will need surgery." Deveney blinked as she looked up, a silent prayer in her heart for her man and his condition. "They don't know how bad yet."

"Come, sit with me." McKala drew her to a chair, watching as Dougal paced and then headed for the outdoors where he knew he would find fellow officers. A female officer, Cate by name, sat beside Deveney. McKala nodded. They were part of a large family, she thought, and they would be taken care of and protected. Not that it helped Deveney in any way.

"He's going to have surgery, McKala. No spinal problems, they don't think but he has internal injuries." Deveney drew in a deep shaky breath. "This sets back the investigation, doesn't it?"

"It may but I know there were others involved with James. The main thing is James and you."

Deveney nodded, her heart too sore to even pray. But she knew that her unspoken words and pleas would be heard. She just didn't understand why and if it was related to what Dougal and McKala were going through.

Chapter 44

Deveney stood at James' bedside late that night. Duncan was beside her, an arm wrapped around his daughter. James was in critical condition, they had been told, and there were no guarantees that he would make it. Deveney wiped at the tears on her face, a hand on James' face, or what she could see for the mask that covered the lower half of it.

"Dad? Why?"

"We don't know yet, Deveney. We have no idea if it is to do with Dougal or not."

"I know that, Dad. I just don't understand it. Why James? Who did he ever hurt?"

"I can't answer that, love. None of us can at the present time." Duncan looked around, hearing the soft sounds of footsteps heading their way. "We need to leave for now, love."

"I know, Dad. This is just not how we planned our day, you know." Deveney bent to kiss her sweetheart and then turned and walked away, not knowing if he would still be alive when she came back. Internal injuries had been dealt with. The physicians had been blunt with her, telling her that he had lost blood and had fractures that would need to heal. Until he awoke, they could not tell if there had been any head injury.

McKala hugged Deveney as she sat back down beside her. She could only imagine how she felt. McKala remembered how she had felt when Dougal had been shot.

"How is he?" McKala's voice was low.

"About the same. It worries me, McKala."

"He'll be sedated for a while. They explained that. He has a long road ahead of him." McKala bit at her lip. "I hate that it may be related to what Dougal and I are going through."

"We don't know that." Duncan spoke up. "I talked to Ted and he said they had to go back through everything."

"I know that, Dad, but it doesn't make it any easier." Deveney's head turned towards McKala. "Where do you stand with the investigation? Do you know?"

"Not really. Dougal was working on that, he said. Others have reached out to him, trying to help. Tag, Evan, and Shay are doing that as are Dooley and someone named Brownie. Abe and Emma are doing the same." McKala sighed. "There is just too much information, I think. It's all working at cross purposes. I can't follow it like it is, on so many different sheets."

Duncan nodded, having reached the same conclusion.

"Abigayle had said the same. She was talking with someone named Micah, who had said he could prepare a program or something like that for us to enter everything into."

———

"Micah? One of Abe's men?" McKala sighed, her head going back. "We are going to owe them so much." She jumped as a hand touched hers and stared at Emma. "Emma? You're here? Where is your son? You should be at home with him."

"It's okay. He's with Abe's Aunt Peg. She adores having him and Isaac adores her. We had to come, McKala, Deveney, when we heard. And you are right. Micah has done what he could for you as has Kat. She has tracked a lot for us, some of what we can't share, but we will share what we can. For tonight, we pray and fast and bring Deveney and James to God."

Deveney and McKala shared a look before they both nodded. Duncan studied the younger women. They're planning something, aren't they, Lord? We have no idea where this is heading but You do. Protect my daughters, Lord. I can't lose either one.

Abe watched the two closely before he shared a look with Emma. They are going to run and run with this as hard and as fast as they can. He watched Dougal as he entered, hesitating before he approached his sister, to crouch down in front of her.

"Deveney? What are they saying?"

Deveney blinked rapidly, thinking that she had cried enough to that day.

"Not a lot. He's critical, Dougal."

"We know, Deveney. The prayer chain is at work. Now, I know you're not leaving. Dad? I'm staying if you want to head out."

Duncan hesitated and then nodded.

<hr>

"I will but I'll be back early. Call me if you need to." He shared a look with Dougal before he hugged his daughter and walked away, fatigue and sorrow weighing down his steps.

"Abe?"

Abe's head turned as his partner, Murphy, spoke from beside him.

"Murphy? You're all set?"

"We are. Their police chief was happy to have our help with Dougal and McKala. He stated that there are officers lining up to protect Deveney and James."

"I thought that. Micah's around?"

"He is. He's heading our way with his laptop, hoping to speak with McKala. I think he needs to wait for morning."

"He will. Right now, those two need to rest, and I know that they won't." Abe turned and walked away, Emma's eyes on him.

"Emma? We will owe you so much." McKala's voice was hesitant.

"No, you won't, McKala. We don't charge friends for this, and you and Dougal are friends." Emma hugged McKala, her eyes on Murphy. "Now, Micah has some stuff for you as we call it but not tonight. Tonight you two get what rest you can."

Dougal rose, taking Emma's spot and just holding his bride. Deveney had moved away, heading for where he wasn't sure, but he saw the

officers and some of Abe's men who followed her.
She would be safe, he thought.

Chapter 45

McKala glared at Micah the next morning, seeing the grin that he was not too successful in hiding. Dougal was not so generous, a wide grin on his face.

"Yes, sweetheart, Micah has information for us. We do need to leave here to look at it." He gently turned her around and headed for the door, Micah keeping step with them, Luke, another teammate of his on their other side.

"I promise, McKala. We'll bring you back." Micah pointed to a large black SUV. "We'll take our vehicle."

"Just like that? We take yours?" McKala was tired and worn out and had had enough of people telling her what to do.

"Yes, ours. Ian's driving. Although if you want, he can take us to the plane and fly you away somewhere no one would find you.'

"That would work." McKala sighed. "I'm sorry. I'm tired of all this." Her hand waved around the vehicle.

"We get that, McKala." Luke shared a look with Micah. "We've been where you two are in a way. And yes, we survived. God provided for us. It wasn't easy, not at all."

———

McKala merely nodded, her head resting against Dougal. She had spoken with Holly earlier and had appreciated the outlook and words of comfort and wisdom that she had been given. Holly was becoming a good friend, one that she needed.

"Can we end this soon?" Dougal watched her face, his question not unexpected.

"We hope to." Luke watched as vehicles moved in around them. "Ian?"

"I know. Dougal, are these your fellow officers?"

Dougal shook his head.

"I don't recognize them." He searched the area. "There. That road on the right. Take it and then take a quick right and then a left. It'll head us back towards the hospital but after two blocks, turn left and keep going. That will head us for the detachment."

Ian's abrupt movement caused consternation in the vehicles surrounding them as he sped away from them, patrol vehicles approaching the vehicles and stopping them. The men were hauled from their vehicles, searched, and then arrested.

Dougal pointed towards the police detachment.

"Head for the back, Ian. They'll let us in." Dougal watched as Ian pulled in behind the detachment and then pulled McKala from the vehicle and into the building. She protested at the abrupt movement, her voice stilling as she saw the look on Dougal's face. It was too close, he thought.

Ted merely pointed to a conference room, heading them there.

<hr>

"What happened, Dougal?" His keen eyes searched the younger man's.

"They surrounded us, Ted. Ian was able to get away. Did patrol move in?"

"They did." Ted didn't say much more but Dougal saw the slight nod and breathed a sigh of relief. At least those men were arrested. "Micah has information I think we'll need. Who's working the case now?"

"Anna is. She had been working closely with James and has stepped up."

Dougal paused for a moment before he spoke.

"Okay. She's away today, though, isn't she? Let us work in here and then we'll come find you or Edward."

"Do that." Ted studied his officer and saw the deep exhaustion that Dougal was feeling. "Dougal? You need to rest. Let Micah work away and then we'll come find you."

"I'm not leaving here, not at all." Dougal sank down into a chair, his head cradled on the arms he had folded on the table. He grew quiet and Ted knew that he was sleeping.

They can't do much more of this, Lord, Ted prayed. *Let us resolve this as soon as we can. And please protect them and the ones around them.*

McKala stood, arms wrapped around herself, staring at the blank white boards. *This isn't working,* she thought. *Okay, so where do we go, Lord? Lead us to find the ones responsible, the bands guys as Camm calls them. Protect those who are working it.*

———

She reached for a marker and started writing. Micah watched her from where he had set up his laptop, his eyes narrowing at the names. *She's good,* he thought. *She knows her town. When we combine what Kat and Emma found with this, we should be closer to a resolution.*

Luke stopped beside Micah, his eyes on Dougal.

"Ian headed back for the hospital. Abe wants us here for now unless we need to leave. And I suspect that we will."

"I am sure that we will. Dougal's crashed."

"He has. It was just a matter of time that he did." Luke studied him and then McKala. "I wonder if he'll continue on the force. His friends didn't."

"No, they didn't but then they were undercover and burnt out. Dougal has been on patrol."

McKala stepped back from the boards, her eyes on Dougal. She sighed. This was taking too much from him, she thought, as she walked towards him, a hand resting on his back. *He was still not back to his full strength,* she thought. *How do we end this and soon? She was determined to end it in the next few days, even if it meant putting herself out there. And she would do that, willingly, she thought. Lord, please?*

Chapter 46

Micah's eyes rested on McKala for a moment before he nodded. She had pinpointed the head one, he thought, the one responsible. But I wonder if she realizes that? He rose from where he had been working and approached her.

"McKala?" Micah watched as her eyes turned to his.

"Micah? Does that help?" She pointed to the board.

"It does, a lot. With what you've written and combined with what Kat and Emma have found, you determined who the leader is."

"I did?" Her brow wrinkled for a moment as she stared at him and then past him at the board. "I didn't know that I had."

"You have. Do you know who it is?" Micah's hand reached to steady as she rose to her feet and headed for the boards.

McKala traced her writing and read what Luke had added at Micah's request. She paled as she reached the end of the boards.

"Him? And mother? I didn't know that." Micah's hand on arm kept on her feet.

"Them. How do you know them?"

———

193

"I don't. I had just seen them around town and avoided them. They had such a manner of evil coming from them. Does God that?"

"Do what, love?" Dougal reached to wrap her in his arms.

"Keep us away from people?"

"He will. He protects us in ways that we don't even know about and won't this side of heaven." Dougal studied his bride and then the board. "Which ones?"

"Them!" McKala refused to say their names, pointing instead at the board. "The son and mother. How are people so evil? And do we even know why? Or what all they were involved in?" Her eyes slid closed and she paled even more. "And they are related to Angus and Austin. Cousins if I remember correctly."

"That helps." Ted spoke from beside her. "McKala, right now, we need you to take a break. Doc Aaron is here at our request. He needs to assess both you and Dougal."

McKala's mouth opened to protest and refuse until she saw the gleam of amusement in Ted's eyes. *He thinks that I'll refuse,* McKala muttered to herself. She shrugged and then headed towards Doc, leaving Dougal snickering behind her.

"You thought that she would refuse."

Ted grinned. "I did. She's something else, you know. Just what you need in your life. Off you go, too, Dougal. Take a break. Don't come back in here for an hour. They've made sure it's safe for you two to be out back in the break area. I hear Abe has sent over two more of his men to be with you."

"He has? Okay then. Off we go." Dougal moved away, his steps still unsteady.

"He's not ready to go back, is he?" Luke's quiet voice had Ted's head turning his way.

"No, he's not. I'm not sure that he will ever be. He'll try it."

"Where can you place him that's not so stressful?" Micah's question had Ted turning to him and then nodding.

"There are some avenues that we can discuss with him. I'm not sure, though, if he'll go for them."

"He will. He's ready to make a change. If not on here, then he'll find something else to do." Micah walked away, heading for his laptop, leaving Ted staring after him.

"He's known Dougal for how long?" Ted turned to Luke.

"It's what we do, Ted. We learn to read people and quickly. Our lives depend on it." Luke walked away on those words, heading for the outdoors to meet with Matt and Joseph.

McKala watched closely as Doc spoke with Dougal, seeing the distress that her husband was feeling. She sighed. *He's determined to protect me, protect Camm and Cori, and everyone else, but his health is just not there.*

"What are you saying, Doc?" McKala moved to lay an arm around Dougal's shoulders.

"He's not ready to go back to work. Not yet. Dougal, you need to recover and haven't."

"I know, Doc, but they need me. McKala needs me to find out who is after her." Dougal was desperate to find the ones responsible.

"We know that, Dougal. I've known you all your life. You are dedicated to your calling. This time, though? You need to step back and let others take over for now."

"I know, Doc. I know that. I just can't." Dougal reached to wrap McKala in his arms, his head buried against her.

Chapter 47

McKala paced the outdoor area, Dougal's eyes on her. He knew that she was thinking, puzzling over the information that Micah had provided to her. She finally dropped to a seat beside him, dejection in her demeanour.

"McKala? Talk to me." Dougal wrapped her in a hug, his chin resting on her head.

"I don't know what to think, Dougal. How did I not know this? And how did Austin get involved in all this?"

"That we'll ask him." Dougal prayed hard for his lady and her family. "Deveney called."

"She did? How's James?"

"Slightly better, they thought, but he has a long recovery ahead of him. Camm and Cori are with Mom and Dad right now. They miss you."

"I miss them too. I need to see them today. Camm's has an insight into the town for one so young."

"I know he does. He's handed over information to us. He said his dad taught him to write things down."

"He did. And Camm does. He has notebooks all over the place. Or at least, he did." McKala fought back the wave of grief at losing her home. "Is that why?"

"Why what?" Micah's voice had her eyes raising to meet his.

"Why the house burnt? Had someone been through it and seen his notebooks? Decided to burn the house down to get rid of them?"

Micah shrugged. "From what I understand, it is still a working investigation. They haven't ruled out anything yet." His eyes met Dougal's. "Did your parents have a locked box or safety deposit box somewhere?"

McKala shook her head. "No, neither one. And there was no safe. So if anything had been documented, it's gone now." She paused, staring past Micah. "Although I do remember Dad muttering something one time. About the garage."

"Was there somewhere in the garage that he would have stored information?"

McKala shrugged again. "There may have been. I guess that means I have to head back there."

"No, not at all. Abe is on his way there now, with Nathaniel and Murphy. They'll look into that for you. All you have to do is give them permission to bring back anything they find."

"They have that. Can I send that in a text?"

"You can." Micah handed over his phone. "Here, it's already for you." He watched with compassion as she sent her text and then hesitated to hand back his phone. "McKala?"

"I remember something. I can't remember who had lend me their phone. It was about six months ago or a bit longer. Just before we went on the run. I needed to find something and someone in my group of friends handed me their phone." She looked up, worry on her face. "I didn't have mine that day. Did I do something wrong?"

"Not necessarily." Ian sat down beside her. "Do you remember whose phone you used?"

"Not really. Three or four people offered me theirs and I just took one. I was too focused on what I needed to find out. And it was so trivial. Just a store flyer for some food." She bit at lip. "Would someone go after me for that? It doesn't make sense."

"No, it doesn't. Think about who was around you that day and try and remember who it was. We can look into that person." Ian watched as McKala turned to him.

"Okay, I can give you the names of who all were in the group. If I go by how we were sitting, I may be able to remember."

Ian jotted down the names as she gave them, his eyes raising and his hand stilling as she stopped speaking.

"McKala?"

"He was there. Austin was there that day. I had forgotten. His was the phone I used. What did I do?" McKala began to shake from fear.

"You did nothing wrong, McKala. We've all done something similar." Ian was on his feet, heading for Ted but his phone out to call Abe. "Abe? Austin is more involved than we thought." he quickly relayed the information.

"He was? That explains it." Abe turned in a circle in the garage. "We're at McKala's. The garage has been tossed, to put it mildly. Does she know where the box would be?"

Ian turned to find McKala standing beside him, Dougal tight to her.

"Ian, when will he be there?" There was a desperation in her voice.

"He's there now, McKala. Only the garage has been tossed."

"Of course it would be." McKala raised her hands, studying them. "Tell him to pull all the drawers from the left side of the work bench. There is a door behind them. There may be something in there. I'm not sure how many people knew of that."

Ian could hear Abe searching and then a quiet "got it".

"Abe?"

"Ian, we're on our way back. Where will you be?"

"Likely at the hospital or their home."

"I would suggest their home. We need to meet. Joseph needs to go over their security once more."

"We can do that." Ian pocketed his phone, his eyes meeting Dougal, who nodded. "McKala, we'll head to your home. Micah has copied everything that you two were working on. Abe's heading back this way."

McKala stared at him, hope in her eyes. "He has it?"

"He didn't say, but he has something or he wouldn't be coming back this way yet. We need to move."

Chapter 48

Abe handed Micah the box that he had been carrying, turning to search for Dougal. Dougal stood nearby, his eyes watchful in his white face. Abe frowned as he saw the dark circles under the other man's eyes. *He's not sleeping,* Abe thought. *He's too worried. We need this over, Lord. How do we protect them? And how do You provide the assurance and rest that they so desperately need?*

"Dougal? You need to be sitting down."

"I know, Abe. I know. It's just.." Dougal's voice died away. "What did you find?"

"I have no idea. We'll go through it but first, where's McKala?"

"In the office, I think. She is determined to solve this today."

"And she may well with what we've brought back. I have not looked at it." Abe's hand steadied Dougal as he turned. "Let's find your wife and then spend some time in prayer. You will need all the protection that God can provide in the next few days."

McKala looked up as Dougal dropped beside her, worry crossing face.

"Abe? What did you find?"

"I don't know, McKala. We'll go through it. But we need to pray and pray hard right now. This is the crisis we've been waiting for and can't avoid."

"I know." She reached for Dougal's hand, finding his warm and tight on hers. "I think Dad knew something but I don't know for sure. He had been researching something or someone." She blinked back tears. "If I had remembered earlier, would we have not had to go through this?"

"We don't know that, McKala. Sometimes God allows events and crises in our lives, to help us trust Him more, to grow. And in your situation, to bring you and Dougal together. He will avenge, McKala and Dougal. Have no doubt about that. Vengeance is God's. He states that clearly in His Word."

"He does. I have to keep reminding myself of that." Dougal stared at the floor, not seeing the dark oak wood under his feet. "It's hard as a human being to trust Someone that you don't see and can't touch to do just that. I still want to be the avenger."

"It is. That's where our faith comes in. I can't promise that nothing more will happen. We can pray that way, but God has already laid this out, before you two were born."

McKala had been watching Abe closely and then she nodded.

"We forget that, don't we? We want to do things our way, charge ahead, and usually into trouble. God wants the best for us, even though it sometimes leads through danger."

An hour later, their heads raised from their prayer time. They all felt refreshed. McKala turned

---

to the box, her hands hesitating on top of it. Dougal just wrapped her in his arms, his chin resting on her shoulders.

"Ian has gone to find something for us to eat. Let's eat first, sweetheart, and then tackle this."

"Okay." She didn't look up, a frown on her face. "Have you talked to your dad? How are Camm and Cori?"

"They're okay. Wanting to be with you but understanding why they can't. They're too vulnerable if they're here. They could be taken and used against you."

"I know but how do we keep them and your parents safe?"

Dougal gave a quick grin. "Ted has off-duty officers with them around the clock. They're with Deveney as well."

"And how is Deveney?" McKala was almost afraid to ask about James.

"She's doing okay. Tired, she says, but James has been awake. They weren't expecting that for a few days."

"No, they wouldn't be. And he'll be anxious to be up and about and working on this."

"He will be but he won't. Deveney won't let him, if I know her."

"They make a really nice couple, do you know that? James has tried so hard to solve this, but I don't think he had all the information that he needed.

———

Someone has been keeping stuff back and I'm not sure who."

Abe had been listening and then approached her, his head tilted to watch her face.

"Why would you say that, McKala?"

"Isn't that what always happens? Someone is on the take, as they say, and hides stuff." She pulled at the tape on the cardboard box. "I just pray that it wasn't me. I don't know if I could live with myself if it was."

Ian and Dougal shared a look, before Dougal gently moved McKala to one side and reached to open the box.

"We don't know what's in here. It may not have anything to do with what we've been going through."

"Somehow, I think it does. I wonder if Dad's accident wasn't an accident after all."

Chapter 49

McKala watched as Dougal carefully turned back the box flaps. Her arms were wrapped around herself. She could hear voices that sounded as if they were coming down a long tunnel, her focus was that intense on the box, wondering what its contents were. Dougal raised his eyes to her face before he reached a hand out and touched it.

"We need to see what is in here, sweetheart. We need to find out who is responsible."

"I know." McKala leaned against him, not listening to the conversation going on around r, or the surprised tones in Abe's voice as he spoke on the phone.

Abe spun to stare at McKala before he pocketed his phone. He approached her, his head tilting to watch her face.

"McKala?" He had to speak more than once before she looked up at him. He drew in his breath at the devastation on her face. "I just spoke with the police chief in your home town. Both Austin and Angus are dead. A drive-by shooting, he said. It appears that they were targeted."

"They're dead?" Hope rose within McKala before it quickly drained away. "Then, what do we do? How do we find out the truth?"

"That we are working on, I promise you. Anna has been in touch with the chief there. Ted is working through it here as well." Abe pointed to the box. "There may be an answer in there. First, though, let's pray once more. You need God's protection on you, both of you."

"I know that, Abe. I just don't feel Him around me. Not any more." McKala stared at the box, not willing to see what was inside, not wanting to know if she could have avoided and prevented what had happened. Only if she had, then Dougal not likely would be in her life. And she needed him. She loved him so deeply, she thought, and knew that her love was returned just as deeply. "How do I know that God is still there?"

"He is, McKala." Dougal hugged her tightly to himself. "He always is. Even when it seems as if He is quiet or not there, He is there. He promised to never leave us or forsake us. He covers us in the cleft of the rock, shelters us in His hands. He has angels all around us."

"He does, doesn't He? It's just so easy to forget that when you're going through stuff." McKala reached into the box at last, Dougal's hands there to take what she was pulling out. "What all did Dad have? I didn't know that he had this."

Dougal glanced through the papers and then stopped at a thumb drive.

"Here, Micah. You take this. See what you find on it."

Micah nodded as he reached for it and then for his laptop. It would take a while, he thought, to sort through what was there, but sort through it he would. He glanced at the files and then drew in a deep breath, his eyes raising to find Abe watching him.

"Abe? It's a lot deeper than anyone thought. Her father has documented a lot of problems and issues with the town and the police force. Even up to higher ranks."

"The chief?" Abe was beside him, studying the file that Micah was researching.

"No, not the chief. But it's close to that." Micah sat back, his eyes on McKala, watching as she and Dougal continued to look through the paperwork. "I have a gut feeling that her father's accident was no accident."

"Somehow, that's the conclusion we have all come to. Now, what do we do about it?"

Dougal spoke from beside him, his eyes on the screen as well.

"Call in Ted. Talk to him first before we go to anyone else. There will likely need to be an outside force called in to investigate. What all were they involved in?"

"That's not clear from this file. I will have to look further." Micah looked up as he felt McKala standing beside him. "McKala?"

McKala had paled as she read the names, knowing that her parents and uncle and aunt had been friends with some of them.

"All them? We knew them. They were friends. Is that how they kept track of us?"

"It would appear so." Micah pulled up another file. "And here is what your dad had found out about them."

"White collar crime? But I don't understand what Dad is saying. It doesn't make sense." McKala rubbed at her temple, a headache starting.

"It will. With what you have given us, we can correlate it with what your father did. And then figure out from there what all crimes are involved. It would appear, though, that they were after the government, lobbying in an illegal manner." Abe stepped back from the desk and paced. He looked up as Ian approached for a quiet word.

Ian headed out, his thoughts troubled by his conversation with Abe. There were men around the house, not from Abe's team. That worried the men protecting Dougal and McKala. It had become very dangerous for them. He shared a look with Murphy, who nodded. The team would work to find the men and take them down. Ted had been called and was sending in officers. Only they didn't know if they would be in time.

$$Chapter\ 50$$

McKala paced that house late that night or rather early in the morning, she thought, glancing at the clock. Dougal had finally crashed, his sleep heavy but disturbed. She had stood and watched him, a hand resting on his hair, prayers raising for his protection. Camm and Cori had called, wanting to be with her. Cori had wept when McKala had simply said that it was too dangerous right now and that they needed to stay where they were.

Moving quietly to the office, McKala stared at the papers that had been taped to the wall. Murphy had simply grinned at her as he and Joseph had done so. Holly and Lincoln had been around and given their two cents' worth. Ted Aaron, a young friend of Dougal's, was even now seated in front of the computer, searching for information.

"Ted? What have you discovered? And you really should be at home." McKala dropped into a chair near the desk.

"This." Ted handed her his work. "It's not as bad as we thought."

"And how did you discover that?"

"By working with what your father had on his thumb drive, with what you've remembered. It's not that many officers. I think your father was listing anyone who might be involved. I set up a database and then sent it on to Emma and Jace. They've sent back a lot of information as well."

McKala sighed as she stared at the work. "And who did you discover is the head one?"

Ted gave a quick grin. "We have. Emma is working to prove it. We'll get this over for you, McKala. I know that it's felt like years and years."

"It has, you know. It has been since Mom and Dad died. Camm and Cori need closure as well."

"We'll get there for you." Ted bit at his lip, a sign of uncertainty. "McKala? Will Dougal stay on the force?"

"I don't know, Ted. I know that is his wish, but it depends on how he recovers."

"What would he do, then? He's always wanted to be an officer." Ted was worried about his friend.

"I have no idea, Ted. We haven't had a chance to really talk about it. There's been too much." She paused, a thought running through her mind. "I don't know what I want to do, either."

"Okay, so you both are uncertain and worried and chased by the bad guys as we call them." Ted grinned as McKala shook a finger at her. "Dad will be around in the morning, he said. He wants to make sure that you two are doing what you're supposed to be."

"I know that he will. And I am grateful." McKala dropped her eyes to the paperwork and then flipped through it, pausing as she caught a name. "Now, how did Emma find him?"

———

"Find who?" Ted stood, reading over McKala's shoulder. "Your dad listed him, with asterisks beside his name."

"He did? I didn't know that. I know that Dad and. Mom avoided him when they could. But what would the town controller be up to?"

Ted's eyes met McKala's and then they grinned at each other, certain that they had discovered their culprit.

"Okay, Ted. Now, let's get started on what we need to list for him. Do you have any information there about his family?"

Ted searched, his eyes raising as he heard footsteps and Dougal appeared in the doorway, hair rumpled and his eyes heavy.

"I do. And here's Dougal to help."

"Dougal? You need to be in bed." McKala spoke absentmindedly, feeling his hand resting on her head.

"I know, sweetheart, but you're in here working away. What have you discovered?" His hand reached for the paperwork, his eyes on her.

"That the town controller was involved. Dad had pinpointed him and Ted discovered it. Emma's sending information as well on him."

"She is? And she won't sleep until she as sent everything that she can."

"She won't? She needs to. Her son needs her as well." McKala became immersed in her reading, not hearing the quiet conversation going on around her, and certainly not hearing Dougal rise to answer a knock at the door. He returned with Ted and Duncan, Abe and Ian trailing behind them.

Chapter 51

Ian stared at the three in the office before he turned, heading for the kitchen. He loved to cook and decided that they needed something to eat to keep them going. Emma looked around at him before she looked past him.

"They're all up?"

"They are. It looks as if McKala and Ted have been working away. Abe will sort it all out. Right now, though, they need some nourishment, just to keep them going."

"I know. Lydia sent some stew and soup that you had frozen with me. That would work."

"It will. Thank you, Emma, for that." Ian worked away, searching for bread and crackers as well. "There. I think this will work."

"It should." Emma reached for the tray with the dishes on it, filled with soup. "I'll take this."

"No, here. Let me. You take the lighter tray." Ian was away before Emma could respond. She just shook her head at him.

McKala looked around, startled to see so many people there.

"Where did you all come from?"

She was on her feet, moving from the room. Finding Emma standing in the kitchen watching her,

McKala stopped. Not sure what to say, McKala hesitated to approach.

"McKala? It's okay. I've been there. This is when it becomes difficult." Emma watched with compassion as McKala struggled to control her emotions.

"I know. I just wish I had known what Dad had found before."

"But you didn't. You had no reason to suspect anything, now did you?" Emma drew McKala to a chair and made her sit. "Now, let's go over what you can remember."

McKala stared at the wall, not seeing the dark cream of the paint, a puzzled look on her face.

"The man that approached me? He works for the controller. I didn't remember that. I just knew he was familiar. He was known around town as muscle for hire or a bodyguard. Why would a town controller need that if he was on the up and up?"

"He wouldn't. That's what we're finding." Emma paused, a thought racing through her mind. "Your father listed a number of people, men and women. Who all of them would be related to the bodyguard or the controller?"

McKala's eyes shot to Emma's and she nodded.

"Most of them, I think." McKala was on her feet, almost running for the office, finding the paperwork that she had dropped. Her sudden appearance drew the men's attention.

"McKala?" Dougal's hand on hers stopped her. "What did you discover, sweetheart?"

"Emma asked who all was related to the bodyguard and the controller." McKala reached for a high-lighting marker, swift strokes marking the names. "The bodyguard is the one who approached me that day. These are all related to either him or the controller or the controller's wife. Now, can we find out why?"

"That we can." Dougal drew her down on the couch with him, Emma on her other side. "Talk to me, McKala."

McKala shook her head, fear running through her.

"This is so hard, you know. I want this over with, Dougal. How do we prove what we know?"

"That's where my team come in." Ted drew up a chair in front of her, his eyes on her. "Young Ted has done great work for us. So have you. Now, we pray, McKala. And then I bring in a new detective who will look at this with fresh eyes."

"Anna?" McKala's eyes slid closed. "She's related, isn't she?"

"Not that we are aware of, but this investigation seems to have stalled on her desk as she is waiting for information. And I will be finding out why. That I promise you."

By the time the dawn light had cracked the eastern sky with purple and pink, they had made a plan. Dougal was not happy with it as it meant McKala putting herself out there.

"We have to, Dougal. By hiding, we're only prolonging it." McKala was adamant that was what she needed to do.

Duncan studied his son and then his son's bride. He sighed to himself. *Yes,* he thought, *Dougal's not happy with that. He knows only too well the danger and the consequences. But I could see Deveney doing the same.*

"We need to support her, Dougal. And we will." Duncan stared down at his son, whose eyes dropped before he finally nodded. "So, how much time do we need, Abe?"

"Not long. A couple of days. Ted, you're going to the paper with a story?" At the chief's nod, Abe looked around. "We keep security on you two, but not obvious. That we can do well. The story goes in to the news outlets today and then tomorrow. It will get back to them very quickly. This is where it becomes very dangerous. This is what we need to do." Abe was frank with them, laying out the various scenarios that they could face, what they could do to mitigate the danger, but also warning them that they were fighting dangerous men and women who really didn't care about someone's life.

Chapter 52

Henry Weatherbee, the town controller in McKala's hometown, shook with rage as he stared at the newspaper handed to him by his secretary. She walked away, not willing to be torn down because of what the article said.

He stared at the article, seeing his name and deeds put out in print. This would ruin him, he thought. He moved rapidly, documents and files locked into his briefcase as he headed for the back door. He was gone before his secretary entered his office again, police officers behind her, warrants in their hands.

Weatherbee slunk through the corridors of the town hall, not meeting the eyes of those he encountered. Many were left to stand staring after him. The article had been read by most of them and they were shocked. But some nodded. They had suspected him for years of buying off government officials to get his way. Justice was coming for him, but who would pay?

He quietly moved towards his car, his bodyguard waiting.

"Where to, boss?"

"Cairn. We need to find that woman and remove her. That should solve this." Weatherbee's thoughts were on how to do just that. McKala would pay and so would those brats that she had as family.

Dougal? Weatherbee shrugged. He was collateral damage as far as he was concerned.

The bodyguard shut the door behind Weatherbee, his eyes on him through the window. He silently shook his head. No, he thought, this won't solve it. Not when it's out in the newspaper. He drove away, heading for Cairn, his thoughts troubled. So far, Gerald thought to himself, he hadn't done anything more than be a driver during the day. His eyes found the rear view mirror and saw the anger and evil that emanated from his employer. Gerald made a decision. As soon as he had his boss somewhere in Cairn, he was done. He would go to the police there and talk with them.

Weatherbee watched as the scenery passed, not seeing the trees and fields and farms as they swept by in a rapid manner. His thoughts were angry. This woman, he thought, had brought down all that he had worked for. His nice little scheme of defrauding the governments and lining his own pocket was over and she would pay. And her cousins would pay once he had dealt with her. Weatherbee plotted and planned all the way to Cairn, walking into the house that he owned there and shutting the door against intruders and the outdoors.

Gerald walked away, heading for the downtown area and the police station as he thought of it. He walked in. The desk officer stared at him and then turned, searching for someone to talk with him. Ted stood an hour later, listening as a detective spoke with Gerald in an interrogation room. This is what we needed, he thought. This will move it ahead.

———

Ted left, heading for Anna's desk, not finding her. A frown covered his face. She had been adamant that she would in the office all day.

"Have you seen Anna?" He approached the desk officer.

"She's around. Did you try the break room?"

"I had. Find her and ask her to come to my office. I need to speak with her as soon as I can." Ted immersed himself in his never ending paperwork as he waited, looking up as he heard a tap at the door. "Anna. Come in and shut the door, please, and have a seat."

Anna sat, her eyes on Ted, a question on her face.

"Ted? You wanted to speak with me."

"I do, Anna." Ted leaned back in his chair, his hands clasped together. "We have an interesting situation there. Are you related to Harvey Weatherbee?"

"Him? Not at all. I know there has been documentation floating around that says that. I asked Mom and Dad. We are related to a Weatherbee but it's not him. There is no family link between us."

"And you have proof, I gather?"

"I do." She handed over a file. "I just finished my report and attached the proof. This is it. I knew that it was being looked at."

"Thank you, Anna." Ted's keen eyes watched her closely. "Now, we have another situation that has just arisen. Apparently, Weatherbee has come back to town. Were you able to determine at all that he owns a home here in town?"

Anna looked at him, shock on her face.

"He does? No, I hadn't found that out. How did you find out?"

"His driver, bodyguard, whatever you want to call him walked in and asked to speak with us. John's interviewing him right now but he will be speaking with you at some point."

"He just walked in? How deeply is he involved?" Anna's mind was racing, her thoughts frightening.

"I am not aware of how deeply involved he is. John will know that. Now, about the investigation? How far along are you?" Ted leaned forward, his eyes steady on Anna.

"Almost there, Ted. Almost there. I am just waiting for some financial reports to come in from the forensics auditor and they will be here this afternoon. He gave me a head's up, and we can nail Weatherbee and whoever it is that he is working for."

"He's not the head one?" Ted was not surprised.

"No, he's not. That Emma had nailed that for us. She's good, you know."

"She is. She and her husband, Abe, had what they call an adventure and from that Emma developed her business. She can't explain how she remembers people and places and events but she is always accurate with them."

"I see. Listen, how is Dougal?" Anna was concerned about her fellow officer.

"Dougal? He's hurting in many ways, Anna. Not the least is the danger that McKala is in."

"I know. I wish this had never happened but sometimes it does, doesn't it?"

Ted smiled. "It does. God allows rain to all on the just and the unjust, on believers and sinners. But He walks through it with us."

Anna nodded, rising, her thoughts deep as she pondered Ted's words. She would need to seek out God, she decided.

Chapter 53

Seemingly on her own, McKala walked the downtown area of Cairn, greeting passersby and stopping to search the shop windows. She had needed to get away from Dougal, if only for a couple of hours. He was starting to hover and smother, and she couldn't have that. McKala knew that Dougal was beginning to feel better and was chafing at the restrictions placed on him.

They had talked, these two, wondering how the newspaper article would be taken by Weatherbee. Dougal was deeply afraid for her, he said, knowing only too well the danger that they had been placed in just by that article. McKala had stared at him and then walked away. She had turned back, her eyes on his eyes, seeing his love for her in them but also his concern.

Deveney watched as McKala approached her before she spoke. McKala jumped in surprise, the stress that she was under making her edgy.

"McKala? You're out and about. Do you have time for a tea?"

"I do." McKala looked around, feeling eyes on her, and then seeing Murphy standing across the street, his eyes not on her but on the people around her. "Where?"

"Here." Deveney pointed to a small tearoom. "This is good. I try to come in here once a week if I can. Mabel is from Scotland and she always has lots of treats that are just so delicious."

"Does Dougal know about this place? He didn't tell me." McKala looked around, feeling someone in the tearoom watching her. "I need to bring Cori here."

"Let's plan on that, if you don't mind me tagging along. I always wanted a sister, but God chose not to allow that."

"We can do that. I know Cori is excited to have you in her life. I miss those two."

"I know. They miss you two, but right now, at the point where you are? They just can't be." Deveney looked around. "Someone is in here watching us."

"I know. I don't think it's Weatherbee but it's likely one of his men. I know Abe has some of his men around."

"He does? I thought that they had all left town." Deveney was surprised at that.

"No, he said that they would be around. I just wouldn't see them."

McKala walked away an hour later, her thoughts troubled. She didn't see Dougal leaning against a store front near her and then walking towards her. Murphy and Ian were approaching her as well, having received word that Weatherbee had found her. A group of teenagers moved into between Dougal and McKala, causing him to stop walking briefly. His eyes sought her and then he was running,

———

trying desperately to reach her but prevented by the movement of the passersby.

"Well, who do we have here?" Weatherbee stopped in front of McKala. His voice caused shudders of terror to run through her as she looked up and then backed away.

"Get away from me." McKala's voice held sobs as she sought for a way to escape.

"Not at all, little lady. You're coming with me." Weatherbee's hand reached out and grasped her hair, pulling her towards him.

McKala fought him, a hand on his trying to release it, and then her other hand hitting and scratching at him. He still dragged her with him, heading for an alleyway. McKala didn't feel the tears of terror that covered her cheeks, unable to scream because of her fear. She faintly heard cries of alarm and then shouts.

Dougal struggled to shove his way through the throng that was heading his way, his eyes on McKala as she was dragged further away from him. He didn't see Ian and Murphy struggling to make their way through the crowd as well or Matt and Nathaniel as they ran towards them from the opposite direction.

Weatherbee shot a look around him, sudden knowledge that he was under attack. He yanked McKala harder and in a more rapid manner with him, heading instead for the road and across it, towards a set of stairs that led down to a lower level and to the river that ran through Cairn. He would drown her, he thought. That would be so appropriate.

McKala dug her heels into the concrete sidewalk as much as she could, her left foot catching in a rough, broken portion and tripping her. She fell forward, the unexpectedness of it sending Weatherbee off balance. They tumbled down the stairs, to lay still, his hand still entangled in her hair.

Matt was down the stairs in almost one motion, on his knees beside McKala. He looked up as Murphy dropped beside him.

"Matt?"

"She's alive and starting to move. We'll need help."

"It's on its way. Ian is keeping Dougal up at the top of the stairs." Murphy looked up, meeting Ian's eyes and seeing his arms wrapped around Dougal.

Ian had reached Dougal just as the younger man had reached the stairs. He had wrapped his arms around him, fighting him to keep him from charging down the stairs. Dougal had finally heard Ian's words and nodded.

"You can't go down there, Dougal. We need to wait." Ian refused to release Dougal, afraid that was the very deed he would attempt.

Dougal nodded, his eyes not leaving McKala, not hearing the shouts and words around him. He didn't see his fellow officers standing around him, for protection and and also privacy. He watched as the town paramedics arrived, working to stabilize first McKala and then Weatherbee. He watched too as the stretchers were wheeled to the rigs waiting below him and then he turned.

<hr>

"I need to go, Ian." He struggled to walk away from Ian, whose hand kept him in place.

"I know you do. Work with us, Dougal. We're trying to protect you."

Abe's men surrounded Dougal, making their way through the crowd to their vehicles and then heading for the hospital. Dougal didn't speak. His heart was praying words that he could not form but he knew that God heard.

Doc Aaron found Dougal an hour later. He had been on duty when McKala had come in. He paused as he studied his young friend, thankful that McKala was not hurt seriously. He traced back through his memories of Dougal, watching in his mind the growth from a baby to the man who sat in the waiting room, his head back against the wall, devastation in his demeanour.

Lord, Dougal is a fine, well-thought of young man, a tribute to his parents but more so, a man of God, who is not afraid to show his faith or to help others. Bless this young couple, Lord.

Doc sat beside Dougal, an arm surrounding Cori as she leaned against him. Camm sat on the other side of Dougal, his eyes on Doc. Worry showed on both of the youngsters' faces.

"Doc?" Cori's soft voice roused Dougal, who blinked rapidly and then looked around. "McKala?"

"She's hurting, Cori. Bumps and bruises. But no broken bones. No concussion. She can go home shortly. First, Dougal? You can head on in to see her. Room 9. I'll be in with these two in a moment or so. I just need to sit and rest my feet for a moment."

"Thanks, Doc. The man?" Dougal really didn't expect Doc to say anything, reading in Doc's face his response. Dougal nodded. "I see. Camm, Cori. Doc won't keep you out here too long." Dougal stood, swaying in his fatigue for a moment before he walked away.

Duncan stared after his son before he turned to Abigayle and Deveney.

"He'll be taking her home. We need to make sure the house is ready for them."

"It is, Dad. Emma's there, she said. I'll head that way." Deveney bit at her lip. "Do you think she's okay?"

"Doc didn't have the look about him that she wasn't. So, I would assume that she is."

Ted stood outside an exam room, watching as Dougal headed for McKala. He turned as Anna approached him.

"Weatherbee is paralyzed." Anna's voice was hushed.

"He is? God has avenged, I would say." Ted stared around, seeing the officer at Weatherbee's door. "We'll keep him under guard. The judge is willing to do his arraignment by video link when Weatherbee is alert."

"He'll have trouble finding a lawyer in town." Anna paused. "God really does care, doesn't He?"

———

"He does, Anna. He really does. Now, off with you. Do what you need to do. I'll be here for a while, I suspect."

Chapter 54

McKala settled down on the couch the next day, Dougal beside her, Camm and Cori on the floor nearby. She was sore, she had to admit, but still worried about Dougal and the youngsters.

"He's not the main one, I don't think, Dougal. There has to be someone else." McKala was adamant that they were missing someone.

"Are you sure? Then, who would it be?" Dougal looked around as he heard the doorbell. "I didn't think that we were expecting anyone."

Camm was on his feet, heading for the door. He opened it, his hands raising as he saw the gun pointing at him. His heart sank. McKala was right after all. There was someone else and they had just appeared. He was spun around and shoved back towards the living room.

Dougal turned as he heard a scuffling sound and started to rise, sinking back and reaching for McKala's hand as he saw Camm returning, a hand on his shoulder to prevent him from running away.

McKala gave a small sound and then anger coloured her face.

"Of course. Adam Weathers. You would be involved. You changed your name years ago, from Weatherbee. How many people have you tried to fool?"

"Enough. Your dad found out and had to be taken out." Adam sneered at her. "And now you will be too. And this house will burn, just like your own did."

McKala's hand tightened on Dougal's. She nodded.

"Of course, it did. You're muscle for hire. Always have been. Weatherbee would have left detailed instructions that you are following. You don't have the brains to think of this on your own."

"You're wrong. I did. Just like your house. That was my idea." Adam didn't catch the looks of disbelief directed towards him by the man with him. "It's all my idea. Weatherbee wasn't the only one who could come up with plans."

McKala stared at him, a frown on her face.

"No, you don't. I know better. Your father is the one who is behind it all. He works for the government. That's who Weatherbee's contact is. And I would say that the detectives have that information. Weatherbee would have left detailed accounts of everything."

Dougal's hand tightened on hers as he saw movement in the hallway. He had heard the quiet opening of the door and knew that someone had entered. Friend or foe? That was the question.

Adam continued to berate McKala, boasting of his deeds. Dougal caught the faint movement of Cori's hand and then smiled to himself. She's somehow managing to record this. Good girl, he thought.

Anna reached for the man standing just inside the living room door, a hand on his arm drawing him back. He was startled and then nodded. It was over, he thought. He would face the consequences of his deeds.

Adam turned at that moment, his gun pointing at Anna and the officers with her.

"I don't think so." Anna's voice was stern. "Drop your weapon."

"Nope. I'm leaving here and she's going with me."

He pointed at McKala, not having heard Dougal rise, his hand reaching for Adam's wrist. A quick movement on Dougal's part and Adam was on the floor, his weapon kicked away from him. Dougal took the handcuffs dangling in front of him and gladly snapped them on Adam's wrists before hauling him to his feet and shoving him away from him.

"That's them all, Anna?" Dougal paused, not quite sure if it was over.

"It is, Dougal. He was the last one that we needed to arrest. Officers in your town, McKala, have arrested his father and his mother for their part in the fraud that they have had going on for years. It will take a while to sort it all out, but as of now, we have everyone." Anna grinned at them. "And James will be so glad to hear that."

McKala was on her feet, wrapped in Dougal's arms as sobs shook her body. Camm and Cori stared at one another and then at Dougal, who simply swept them into a group hug. Anna watched for a while before she turned. Officers would stay for now, talk

———

to the quartet, and then leave. Crime scene techs would be around but not for long.

McKala leaned back to look up at Dougal, her arms around her cousins.

"It's over?"

"It is, sweetheart. It is. And now we can go on with our lives. This calls for a celebration."

Camm's arm pumped the air and then he hugged Dougal.

"What kind of celebration? And who all is here?"

"We'll plan something for everyone in a day or so but for now, it's just us four. What can we do?"

"We need to be outside. Is there somewhere fun we can go and have a picnic?"

"There is. There's an old quarry outside of town that has been turned into a park and picnic area. Race you to get a meal ready." Dougal grinned as Camm and Cori shouted with glee and then ran for the kitchen. He looked down at McKala who had moved back into his space and simply bent and kissed her thoroughly. "I love you so much, sweetheart. I was so afraid that I would lose you."

"I love you too, Dougal. God has been good. You wanted to be my avenger but God has been that. He led you as well in your quest to vengeance but vengeance has been His."

Epilogue

Six months had passed. Weatherbee had been arraigned with numerous charges, not the least was attempted murder and conspiracy to commit murder among those charges. Adam and his parents were also charged with a multitude of charges. Anna had been around many times, the last the day before. She had sat with McKala and just talked, not so much about what McKala had been through but how she had coped. Anna was seeking to grow in her walk with the Lord and felt that McKala would be the best one to speak with.

McKala had shared what she had been feeling, her doubts, her joys, her sadness, her fears. She had been open with Dougal as had he. They had grown close, this young couple, closer than they might have been under unordinary circumstances. Dougal had simply grinned when McKala had asked if he thought that they might have met otherwise. His only comment was that God knew all along that they were meant for one another and that He had known what they would go through.

Dougal was back at work but not on the streets. He was disappointed not to be there, as he had loved his contact with the people of his town, but accepted the post of detective. He hadn't been sure of that when he had been told to put in for it, but he and McKala had prayed about it. Both were confident that was where he was to be.

Camm and Cori had been quiet for a number of weeks after their adventure, as they called it. McKala had found someone for them to counsel with and that had helped. Dougal had taken on the role of big brother to them and his gentle words, his prayers, his guidance, and his admonition were all taken in the spirit in which he offered them.

James had healed and he and Deveney were planning a wedding in the next few months. He had apologized to McKala that he hadn't been the one to finish the investigation. McKala had simply shaken her head and told him that it had been taken out of his control. Anna had done just fine in his place.

That day, McKala looked around as she heard Dougal's footsteps. She frowned as she looked at the clock. He was home early, she thought.

"Dougal?" Her face rosy from his kisses, she leaned back in his arms to look up at him.

"McKala? Mom and Dad have asked that we come for dinner today. They want us dressed up. Apparently, Camm and Cori are already over there." He grinned down at her.

"They are? I thought they were up to something. Did your Mom say why?"

"Nope. Just asked that we be there."

Her hand tight in his, Dougal and McKala stepped through the door into Duncan's home, hearing the sound of happy voices, laughter and soft music. Duncan watched his son and his wife, thankful that they were relatively unscathed from their adventure. He knew there were days that it hit hard and those days were becoming fewer and fewer.

"Dad? What's going on?" Dougal's eyes narrowed as he saw his father trying hard to hide a smile.

"Just a celebration for you two." Duncan's arm came around Abigayle. "We know that you didn't have a wedding like you deserved and then faced life and death situations right away. What we want to do is not interfere. We know that you don't want to renew your vows. You both have said that on numerous occasions. What we would like to do, though, is just celebrate with you. Our friends are here. Our church family is here or will make their way through over the night. We just wanted to do something for you, to help make new memories for you both."

Dougal and McKala exchanged glances. This was not what they had expected. McKala blinked back tears as she reached to hug the couple that she thought of as Mom and Dad.

"Thank you. It does help."

McKala stood in the yard late that night, the darkness of the sky broken by the twinkling stars and the light of the full moon. The solar lamps around the yard were in full display. Dougal watched her from his post near the back deck, amazed that she was his. She is so beautiful, he thought, and she's mine. He moved towards her, wrapping her in a hug.

"Okay, sweetheart?" His voice was low but held the love he felt for her.

"I am, my love. I am. Your parents didn't have to do this, but I am glad that they did. We needed this."

"We did. And they were so glad to do it."

They stood, lost in thought, watching their friends and family moving around them.

"Are you okay with being a detective, Dougal? It's not what you wanted."

"Not it's not, but it's where God wants me. Until He says otherwise, I stay. What about you? Have you decided what you want to do yet?" Dougal knew that McKala was struggling to find something to do.

"No, not yet. Holly has asked me to work her office for her as has Lincoln. Both are just so busy with their work. Doc has asked if I want to work in his office." She sighed, not sure what she wanted to do.

"But you're not sure, are you? Just take your time. But that's not all."

"No, it's not. Camm and Cori have settled in well."

"They have. You have done well raising them."

"They have been easy to raise. They don't challenge me like some do." McKala's head rested against Dougal. "I heard from the real estate agent. My property has sold. I was planning on telling you tonight."

"I'm glad. That gives closure on that."

"It does." McKala bit at her lip. "Dougal? What if we have our own family? We haven't really discussed that, not yet."

"No, not yet. It's something I guess that I thought we'd consider in the future." He paused. "Are you telling me something?" He felt her nod and tightened his hug. "You'll make a real mother, sweetheart." His head bent over hers.

"And you a father. It's not for about seven months. Can we wait to tell?"

"We can, sweetheart. I love you."

"And I love you. You truly were my avenger, sweeping in to rescue me, helping me, being the man God had chosen for me. God's vengeance is there as well. We forget that He does avenge."

"He does. We don't always see it but it's there."

They stood, lost in their love for one another, their thoughts deep. Duncan and Abigayle watched them, before Duncan spoke.

"They went through so much, Abigayle, but stood true to God and to one another. I'm not sure that we would have picked the one for the other but God's ways are best."

"That they are. She completes him and he her. If she wasn't in our lives, we wouldn't have Camm and Cori. I would have missed a lot not having them as family."

"That we would. Now, let's just spend some time in prayer for our family. It's growing, dear."

"It is." Abigayle studied McKala and then smiled to herself. She had a good idea that the family would be growing even more. *God, You have blessed us. Continue to lead in our lives.*

Dear Readers:

Thank you for choosing to read The Avenger. It has taken a long time to write. McKala and Dougal were not really forthcoming with their story. McKala's name was originally Carragh, but she refused it, making me change it to another. Once that happened, then the story unfolded.

God as an avenger? Have you ever considered that? It does state in His Word that vengeance is His and that He will repay. We may never know on earth what He has avenged for us, but rest assured, if He says that He will, He does.

As I finish this novel, it is mid-fall here in Ontario. I enjoy the changing of the seasons, even though winter is approaching. It reminds me of how our lives change as we move through the seasons of life. Dougal and McKala are in the summer of their walk together. The characters always drive the story. And I love it when old friends walk back in, just as Abe and his team did. Their adventures are in the *His Guardian* series. They always seem to move the story ahead as well.

God bless each one of you. Keep your hand in His. He knows the ways that we walk and has since the foundation of time.

Ronna

www.ingramcontent.com/pod-product-compliance
Lightning Source LLC
Chambersburg PA
CBHW061241210726

48293CB00003B/858